Bogotá

BOGOTÁ

A NOVEL

ALAN GROSTEPHAN

TriQuarterly Books
Northwestern University Press
Evanston, Illinois

TriQuarterly Books
Northwestern University Press
www.nupress.northwestern.edu

The epigraph, from *Herzog* by Saul Bellow, was printed with the permission of
The Wylie Agency LLC. Copyright © 1964, 2003 by Saul Bellow.

Printed in the United States of America   JAN 2 4 2014

10 9 8 7 6 5 4 3 2 1

This is a work of fiction. Characters, places, and events are the product of the author's
imagination or are used fictitiously and do not represent actual people, places, or events.

Library of Congress Cataloging-in-Publication Data
Grostephan, Alan.
    Bogotá : a novel / Alan Grostephan.
       p. cm.
    ISBN 978-0-8101-5230-4 (pbk. : alk. paper)
    1. Bogotá (Colombia)—Fiction. 2. Bogotá (Colombia)—Social conditions—
Fiction. 3. Rural-urban migration—Colombia—Fiction. I. Title.
    PS3607.R6744B64 2013
    813.6—dc23
                                                                    2012039872

∞ The paper used in this publication meets the minimum requirements of the American
National Standard for Information Sciences—Permanence of Paper for Printed Library
Materials, ANSI Z39.48-1992.

For the people of Cazucá

and for María

No life so barren and subordinate
that it didn't have imaginary dignities,
honors to come, freedom to advance.

—Saul Bellow, *Herzog*

CONTENTS

Part I

Home

3

Part II

The Capital

51

Part III

The Future

123

Acknowledgments

229

BOGOTÁ

PART I

Home

CHAPTER ONE

MORE THAN A KNOCKING, it was a clicking. Not metal on wood or metal on metal but a tongue flicking against the roof of a mouth. No, it was softer, the hand of a man certain of the power he kept over another man's house. Because no one ever knocked in this town—they knew better, they spoke your name through a gap in the boards—but these, the hoods.

Wilfredo placed a worn piece of cardboard over his shoulder onto which he raised an outboard motor that had been leaning beside the television. Alba was staring at his feet in the dark. She was pregnant and held her hands curled up against her belly, as if to catch water or a piece of food from rolling down her chest to the floor. What might she say? What might he? To say the word *luck* or *help* or *stay* would only put that word into question.

"Stay," she said. "Your motor is broken."

The hoods followed Wilfredo down to the river's edge, their rifles swinging from their necks as they climbed into the bow of his fiberglass boat. They pushed off into the current toward the white walls and canoes of Puerto Clavel, not using the motor yet, just the paddles, and in this way Wilfredo faced his own town, Cuturú. It looked peaceful enough tonight with two streetlamps shining over orange brick houses on four streets, but it was a rotten town. The tallest building was the police station, freshly painted but abandoned, with its red antenna, its razor wire looped high over layers of sandbags. A year ago, the guerrillas burst through the front door, chained the policemen by their necks, and walked them into the mountains. Briefly, it was a guerrilla town. At the hottest part of the day, when beer went warm after a sip, the paramilitaries retook it and tried to hang the traitors from makeshift gallows but ran out of rope and ended up shooting them many times and tossing them into the river.

Wilfredo jumped off the side, dragging the panga onto the muddy ledge of Puerto Clavel's port and waited while the hoods disappeared over the embankment. There were no streetlamps, and it was hardly a town, on the wrong side of the river with no roads, and whatever happened was concealed by trees and white shacks. He didn't want to know. He heard nothing. He stood at the stern of the panga, both feet in the water, making sure his motor was screwed on tight.

The hoods returned with three teenage boys, all of them puerto-claveños Wilfredo knew in passing but could not name. He helped them over the gunwales, as he did all clients, while the hoods pushed them facedown into the cross-bracings of the bow.

The motor, cold, cold, cold, refused to start. Wilfredo slid the choke in, squeezing the rubber fuel bulb until it was firm. He removed the cover and looked at the wires, the gears, pulled out the sparkplugs and blew on them, wiped them clean on his shirt. He could fix anything. Some days, though, he sweated over the motor in the sun while his clients watched, and he would have to unclamp it and carry it back to the patio workbench where, among the biting black flies, away from the eyes of his neighbors, he broke down—it was a beautiful fifteen-horse Yamaha.

The motor sputtered and worked up a steady rattle, and they were launched out into the deep center of the river. The half-asleep of Puerto Clavel and Cuturú, facing each other diagonally across el río Puerco, must have awoke to the noise. He looked back across the water, yellow from the sodium used to treat gold upriver, and saw Alba in the port, watching him the way he hated, as if it were his fault.

Pointing him upriver from the bow sat a half-hooded man who tried to hide his farmer's hump by tilting his head backward, as if someone were pulling him by the ears with two hands. He was el Suizo, the paramilitary first brought in by the gold companies to protect their land from the guerrillas, nicknamed for his hairless, monumental head, and his skin, despite the tropical sun, as pale as snow. His head was so big that when he wore sunglasses they would pop off in the wind, and his body, despite his self-conscious efforts, slumped sideways under its weight, so big and with so little inside it but a simple seed of malice. When he sat next to you at a table in the cantina you could not get up. When he came to piss next to you in the alley you could not turn away as he eyed your dick and made a joke about it.

Next to him, jabbing his toe into the neck of one of the boys, the barrel of his rifle on the head of another, tapping it slightly against the boy's scalp, sat Mamita. It was a fair nickname, as he had a propensity to pull out his bull dick, a veiny trunk of pink, and set it on the table when he was drunk and scream, "Mamita!" Some said he slapped you with it before he killed you or that he attached a blade to the head of it and bushwhacked through the forest or that he dipped it into the river as a depth finder for fish, but Wilfredo knew the truth. He liked young farm girls. He drove fathers in the region crazy, forcing them to send their daughters away to the city. Of the ten or eleven paramilitaries who got paid by the gold-mining companies to spend time in Cuturú, he was the hardest to live with, and although Wilfredo wanted one badly, he paid the shaman so Alba would not give birth to a daughter.

Nights were different in a thousand ways. Wilfredo could feel the whole basin, the tributaries, the shallows, the windfalls of last year rotting in the warm water, taking order in his mind. He did not have to see; these night errands for the devil were his curse for knowing. He moved them upriver slowly, the panga riding low under their weight. Owls and night birds cut black dashes through the trees. He steered wide from each village, some canoes beached here, a few buoys to mark nets, even though everyone recognized the sound of his motor.

After an hour, the towns tapered off. Near the entrance of a little tributary named el Tombito, they came to a small beach on the paramilitary side of el río Puerco where a man waited in a hammock with no hood on his head but a chainsaw at his feet. His face looked like an armpit, his big red lips puffed out, some black wiry stubble on his chin, his cheeks loose with reddish creases. He too had lighter skin, and his was a saintly face, straight from one of the religious lottery posters in the chapel, yes, a friendly face, as if nothing it had seen had done it much damage. He helped Mamita and el Suizo dig knee-deep holes for the heads of the three boys who, now, in the thick laurel silence and darkness of a little nowhere beach, denied having any involvement with the guerrillas. The holes were to suffocate and gave the men leverage. They pulled back their hoods entirely, for this was work.

After a while they pronounced the first boy dead. Ejected from the sockets, his eyes hung on slack cords. Night birds cackled; crickets roared in terrific rhythm.

They buried the live breathing head of the second teenager and hammered down on his spine with the butts of their rifles, prying his head out of the ground for a question, then shoving it back in. Wilfredo heard what he assumed was nonsense about the guerrillas' position, the location of certain coca fields, names of narco contacts, routes on the river, some lies everyone knew. By the third boy the men were tired. They drank. They pulled through a liter of aguardiente and opened a second bottle. They set up the bodies on homemade sawhorses and cut them in half with the chainsaw, then the arms, then the legs, then the heads and feet. They opened the torsos so the bodies would sink. Though softer than wood, the bodies were already stiffening, the saw jammed at the bones, and the men struggled to make clean cuts. Diarrheic feces and urine wormed through their boots. They stripped off their hoods, and the liquid innards sprayed out onto their chests and faces. When they were done, they tossed most of the flesh into the river. They were not laughing. They waded into the water and scraped at their own skin with their fingernails. They swayed, clumsy in the current. They put the dismembered feet into the bow of the boat and said farewell to the man with the chainsaw who was already climbing back into the woods.

Some rain fell. It was the wet season, the river high and deep. Wilfredo's feet were caked in mud. In the dry season, you could almost jump across the river, and it smelled like manure. They would make fires down by the water and cook sancocho for the fiestas, praying and toasting to the guardian saints. He wondered if this was his last run. He saw the river fine in the rain. The thick laurel on the shore picked up light from somewhere, a vague glitter. He tried to fool himself that it was one more errand on any night, a pregnant woman or an ill child needing to go to Bagre, perhaps on credit never to be seen as cash; they might pay him in yucca or a decent hen or a bag of vegetables—a delicacy here where they did not grow. But every time he took his eye off the river, he saw the hoods perched on the gunwales with their bottle of aguardiente, which was not offered to him, and in the bottom of the boat, not bleeding, not even calling for attention, the severed feet of the boys.

At the port in Cuturú, the men put their hoods back on and swallowed what was left of the bottle. They offered it to Wilfredo, waist deep in the river, scrubbing the blood from his boat. The rain helped. He would try to get some cargo for tomorrow, to absent himself and his family for a few days and take Alba, who was eight months pregnant, to the clinic in Caucasia. But first he would sit on his patio until the sun was up. He would walk through town to the grocery store as usual. That was the way to handle it. People knew him. He had always been good.

CHAPTER TWO

PADRE MOISÉS HAD AWOKEN that night at the first sound of Wilfredo's motor sputtering to a start across the river, the only new fifteen-horse Yamaha in town. Otra vuelta, he thought. Another errand. Soon there'd be a voice at the door asking him to come out.

Who is dead? el Padre would ask.

No light penetrated the dirty windows of the chapel. The whole building leaned bright white in the main square of Cuturú, neighbored by the cantinas, the butcher shop, the grocery, and the abandoned police station with its high red antenna with no signal. Closed shops everywhere, vacant houses, missing roofs, and this meant his parish was dying. Sure, the gold companies were still dredging the river, digging everywhere along the floodplain. Fish survived despite the pollution; coca grew, it grew better than anything else, no matter how many times they sprayed and uprooted it.

El Padre often drank hot coffee with Alba in the worst heat of the afternoon. Near dark, as the day cooled down, they would eat together, and because their house stood overlooking the port, he usually found himself sitting at the bench in front of it. He gave books to their youngest son, steered wide of the oldest, and would do anything for Alba, whose sad eyes and missing chin drew her close to him as the misery of women always did. But tonight, because of the fleas in the chapel, he felt too selfish to do more than sit up in his bed. The poison had not yet arrived and around the veins in his hips and legs, standing naked in the bathroom mirror, he had counted sixteen bites. He could feel them jumping up into his bed. His blood was too sweet, and although they said it would adjust over time, as fleas did not really thrive in the tropics anyway, his had not.

His stay here would be short, as had been and would be that of all priests in parishes where coca grew. Lately, though, he was shocked to hear himself singing along to the lusty and violent ballads of Cuturú, swinging his one arm for balance. Right there in la plaza de Bolívar, next door to the cantina, the paramilitaries had run a coca laboratory until a month ago when the military passed through with no real purpose, spraying down with poison certain coca fields to the east and taking pictures of themselves doing it. They politely asked el Suizo and his men to stay out of sight. Everybody was after the same land, the same money; the paramilitaries paid the guerrillas to move product, and the military paid the paramilitaries to hunt guerrillas, and the guerrillas paid off the military in order to move their product. When the bluevest UN peace mission had come in to ask el Padre if the paramilitaries were acting autonomously, he laughed at them. They do the dirty work, he said, but they share beds and guns and women, and all the men with guns are the same man and they love each other. The bluevest, with a Swede's blue eyes and a Swede's eager frown, wrote all this down and said he'd report it. To the great peace committee of the world that had no power, no testicles.

He sat out in the courtyard to breathe in the cooling air, its taste of pine and river, and he dozed a little knowing it would not do to sleep here, but then he did, dreaming his hand was drenched in poison he thrust into the river.

"Padre! Padre! Despiértese!"

"Who is dead?" Padre Moisés said, surprised to see the fat sister of a campesino who lived an hour's walk into the hills. She looked at his one hand scratching hard at the veins in his hips.

"He's close to leaving us," she said. "There was an explosion in his stomach."

"Who? And the motor?"

She looked confused.

"Vamos," he said. "Let's walk by the port and see if Wilfredo has returned. He can take us upriver. It's shorter."

El Padre paused to look at Alba in the candlelight of her kitchen, but this other woman was pushy, pointing downriver, not wanting to hear or see or know any of it, so they left town in the dark.

CHAPTER THREE

AT AGE THIRTEEN, Hernán did not antagonize or disobey like some unhappy children but kept his sorrow hidden. Like his father Wilfredo, he spent most of his days alone, in the woods or in the empty hills, digging for guaca. Guaca was treasure, and he was a purist in that he dug for anything—indigenous artifacts, drug money, weapons, gold—but his greater wish was to find a dinosaur bone. When he wasn't digging, he helped Wilfredo, and already had a good feel for the river, but the river would not be for him. That was decided. This year he would finish the elementary school, and they would send him to study in Caucasia. If he wanted to be an engineer, as Wilfredo wanted, to dig things for real profit, to have an office, a truck, a hardhat with the emblem of one of the gold or oil companies, he would have to go.

Hernán trusted Cuturú because he knew where things were. He knew Wilfredo was downriver and Alba was standing at the stove, watching white blobs of yucca boil in water, that she wore the yellow cotton dress with red palms, that she loved him and wondered why he was not up yet, and that Milton was smoking in the doorway, watching the river for a sign. They kept space between each other. The power had just blinked out for the rest of the night, maybe longer, and so a candle was lit.

"Was it el Suizo again?" Hernán said, and watched Alba spoon coffee into a cloth filter. He touched her stomach, wondering if the baby could be bored. She did not answer, so he picked up the manual for the Yamaha and studied the diagram of the motor's innards.

Milton roamed the small kitchen and was everywhere. He seemed naked in the candlelight, his lower body in darkness, his tattoo of a long blue harpoon running from his shoulder to his wrist.

"Stop," Alba said. "Go outside if you have to move so much."

"Let's go," Milton said.

He and Hernán crossed the street to the port, through the canoes and boats tied down to eyelets in the mud, and waded into the river. Even this low, the current was fast—one step too far and it took you. Hernán leaned beneath the surface to listen for the buzz of a motor but only quiet water pushed against his ear. The houses were dark on both sides of the river, but he could hear whispers and the occasional striking of a match. No one could sleep when someone was taken.

"When?" Hernán said.

"I don't know," Milton said. "Soon."

"You said that before. And what would papá do in the city? Drive a taxi?"

Milton smoked hard, his throat seeming to bleed and his lungs aching from something. Hernán was the smart one, the one who could solve any math problem, who read over your shoulder, but Milton too was planning to leave—maybe south to Medellín, where any pendejo, people said, could get lucky. Milton had once longed to sit with the children in the blue school and hear Padre Moisés speak about long division, botany, the Spanish Colony, but when they decided you were the son without a brain you had to accept it, never taking notes or raising your hand or telling people you were digging for dinosaur bones. It meant you were stuck on four streets, dipping your face into a polluted river, riding through the green hills with a cigarette. You waited for something to happen to you. It would. Even with el Suizo running the town, the guerrilleros would come back for him. The first time, Wilfredo had some money and told them he needed his son's labor for the business. He paid the tax. He lied. But what do I care? Milton thought. What do I know? Some nights he went into the woods, despite the mosquitoes, and jacked off to a postcard of a beach in Cartagena, or he dragged Lucila, one of the ugly farm girls in with him, telling her what to do, saying, Te amo, te amo, to keep her going. He had punched her once in the neck for flirting with a guerrillero, but she liked it, thinking he had found his pride. He had not. Even when he snuck off to get the harpoon tattoo in the city, he failed. The tip was no longer sharp, the blue running into the black, and soon it would look like a long shapeless fishbone.

Milton posed as a man. But even at church, the other men sized him up in a glance. Every word he spoke, "Una cervecita, por favor," they measured, and so Milton smoked too much, spit over his shoulder when he walked places, and turned his whole body, not his eyes or head, to look at women. But that was not enough. People knew. The paramilitaries were not interested in him. He was meat for the guerrilleros who would recruit anyone and keep him for life.

"Maybe he went downriver," Hernán said, trying to take Milton's cigarette from him. "Maybe they just needed more supplies in Bagre."

"He went upriver," Milton said. "I heard it. I was never asleep."

"Why?" Hernán said.

"We're going to Bogotá. I'm sure."

"Chicos, come inside," Alba said, whispering. "Everyone hears you. Basta!"

A mosquito flew through a gap in the screen door, and Alba slapped her cheek, streaking it with her own blood. She sat and stood and tried to eat yucca and sat and stood. She was a superstitious woman, and all the signs were sinister tonight. It was not unlike the night they took her father who used to drive a taxi between here and Caucasia, who had the guts to say no to the paramilitaries, no ride, no favors, he was neutral, his business depended on it, and they undressed him in the hills for death. Her father did not frequent the cantinas or drink water from the new aqueduct, but preferred the water from the river, joking that he was worth his weight in the gold he had swallowed over the years. She saw the simple punctures of a drill through his eyes and forehead, and she breathed now, standing, as if just coming to the surface, every object in the house sharply defined and peculiar. She ate fresh, salty cheese from the warm refrigerator and sprinkled salt on a piece of boiled yucca. She carried it behind the bedroom curtain, the same pattern as her dress, which she pulled up now to find a spot of blood in her underwear. The baby was moving around, trying to stand perhaps, afraid already and it had not even opened its eyes.

A light trickle of rain became a pounding on the zinc roof. A line of water ran through a crack in the ceiling, but no one moved to fetch the bucket.

*

Hernán woke to the smell of the hot gears and burned oil of the Yamaha, a puddle of river water forming beside the television. Wilfredo nodded at him and was telling Alba that he had to go up the road with the men but that he would be back by the afternoon. Behind him, Hernán saw nothing but the yellow river, the panga in its place. Wilfredo looked at each of them and at the house as if to remember it. His voice came out dry and without enough air to carry his words. Bogotá, his voice said without saying; he squeezed Alba's hand, and his eyes said, Pack. He shut the door on himself.

Milton looked out through a gap in the wall to see what direction they took and said, "Go tell Padre Moisés."

On his way to the plaza, Hernán smelled coffee, some brewing and some burning, and eggs being fried in oil. He looked at the closed doors of his neighbors and knew that he had seen this moment before. Not in his house. Others kids gone looking for the priest.

Across from the chapel hung bright red Coca-Cola posters, and a long yellow gasoline tank stood in the doorway of the grocery, the dusty bottles of rum in their rows, the boxes of candy and packaged chocolate-covered cakes—things Wilfredo had delivered in his panga and had probably not been paid for yet. Dark inside, there was still no power. A few campesinos from downriver were buying cooking oil and batteries and gasoline, loading it all onto carts or the backs of their mules. They had come early, when usually they would be milking their cows. They seemed bothered, checking across the river to see if anything moved in Puerto Clavel. A gray mule laid huge smug eyes on Hernán's. Outside one cantina idled a yellow taxi from Caucasia.

Hernán crossed the street to the chapel and pushed on the locked door. "Padre!"

"No está," said the grocery owner, his hair in bright curls of silver, his face oily, flat, like a long calculation. He looked across the river at Puerto Clavel, where blue smoke hung from rusty brown roofs and the white canoes were still beached and upside down. "He went to Socorro to see a sick campesino. What happened?"

CHAPTER FOUR

THE WOODS HELD BACK the cool river valley breeze, and soon Wilfredo and the hoods were sweating, passing through half-macheted bushes and wet laurel, too tired to slap the mosquitoes from their necks and ankles. He knew this landscape, but today the green hills looked foreign. He imagined his body thrown piecemeal, footless, into the thick brush and never found.

At a rise, the hoods stopped for breath. The sun cleared the trees and lit up the yellow elbow of river below. They pulled off their hoods and undershirts, and like this, bare, bony, became regular men, slightly drunk. Both were outsiders from the coast, sent down from Montería, and while Mamita was rude, his mouth full of spit he dribbled on anyone's floor, el Suizo was often friendly and occasionally bought a suspicious round of beer at the cantina.

Wilfredo was a slow and clumsy walker. For this, on deliveries to the hills, he usually sent Milton who bitched endlessly about the rusty cart, yet happy to show off his new tattoo and gossip with campesinos about what he knew, which was nothing.

Throwing his head backward to seem a confident military official and not a campesino, el Suizo preached to Wilfredo about the failures of the Colombian national soccer team, how they had scored the first goal against Brazil, and the hope it had given him, but then those Brazilian giants, so fast, so fluid, so aware of one another and of space, geniuses, he pronounced them, as if dancing and not running, without sweat or worry, scored two goals, then a third. And it was one thing to lose to the giants or unfairly to the Bolivians in La Paz, gasping for breath a mile above sea level, but a disgrace to lose to Venezuela, a baseball country. Inexcusable, he said. The problem, for he had spent time thinking about it, bored in his hut in Turbai, waiting for orders, was that every player played for himself. They could not know space like that, like the Brazilian giants. That's why you would have to kill the whole team and start from zero.

Wilfredo agreed. "Perhaps it is the chemistry."

"Perhaps?" el Suizo stared at him, baffled. "Perhaps?"

They were passing through the rusty steel gates of a large hacienda, abandoned seven years ago when the guerrillas had kidnapped the owner and his horse. A draft of fish frying came from the white stucco house with flaky purple balconies. A columned doorway was blocked by a high pile of sandbags and a circle of razor wire, which had been cut. At one of the side doors sat an indigenous man mending a sandal, and Wilfredo imagined the mansion to be full of them. The front yard banana trees were sick with some brown rash on the trunks, and the fruit hung rotten. Out in the first field, they passed some campesinos digging rows of yucca, and approached a small grouping of huts on stilts.

"Sober?" Mamita said. "I feel like shit."

"I don't know," el Suizo said. "Is there another bottle? Mierda. No, there's not." He looked around for a supermarket and saw only the still rows of palm trees. "We could send one of these indios?"

Tied by one ankle with a piece of twine to the front step of a larger, newer hut, a rooster was pecking at a dog turd. He looked sullen, hungry, and seemed to recognize Wilfredo, kicking his heels into the ground.

"Sale!" el Suizo said, leading them up the stairs.

Inside, he told Wilfredo to sit at a table, served him cold coffee and a bowl of plain rice, and apologized for the weak portions.

Mamita looked for a bottle but turned up only empties, and then hurried behind a florid plastic shower curtain to take a shit. When he was done, he stripped to a tight pair of black underwear, his large penis poking out the side, and laid down on a bright blue and red beach towel on the floor. El Suizo pointed and called it the trunk of an elephant, told him to tuck it in. Then he cleaned the rifles, and strung up a hammock for his own rest. Neither slept. They looked up with wide open eyes, as if the sooty wood ceiling were a tapestry being woven day by day of the exploits of two drunken men in hoods whom they knew fairly well.

"The thing is," el Suizo announced to no one, "men don't like pain."

It was the terrible, post-rain heat. You could smell it in the boards, as if the paint were burning up. Outside the air turned to steam. Cotton-swab clouds clumped together above the trees. The machine of insects that broke every night and followed a familiar tune all day was in full force, a humming rising to a high pitch until the clouds momentarily covered the sun. All went silent, even the birds. Wilfredo shut his eyes and then opened them to look at his feet. His toes seemed longer than normal, the veins bulged out, one of his toenails gone, and the others, fractured and overgrown, had taken on the yellow of the river.

Around noon, el Suizo received a call on his cell phone. He had to climb up onto the roof to get better reception. When he came down, he told Wilfredo he could either stay here or take his chances. If he went home, he was to wait until tonight. They would need him again. "Why not wait here where it's safe, Panguero?" he said. "It's my advice, hermano."

The men, shirtless, reddened by the heat, slung their rifles and walked up the road toward Caucasia. The rooster had tangled himself up in the cord, moving his red-lumped head from side to side as if seeing his hunger everywhere.

Wilfredo walked out to the path without glancing at the abandoned splendor of the hacienda and passed a campesino with giant white teeth and a gray chicken feather behind his ear. He was hauling a sack of dirt, looking sideways at the sun.

"Wrong way," the campesino said. "I know you. They grabbed your son, Panguero."

"Who?"

"In Cuturú there are puertoclaveños. The whole town, it seems. They're all in the port."

Past the mansion, the indios had come out to stare at a sick cow. Wilfredo found himself running for the first time in years. He had waited too long to escape Cuturú. Everyone always left too late. He had walked the streets and eyed the looted, empty houses, and kicked dirt over their blood, and then he made the same mistake. He ran in the way of the frightened, bringing his knees up too high, reaching out farther than he should have with each stride, his hands striking at the brush. He caught his foot on a root and slid on his back down one of the steeper slopes along the trail. No time to consider the spectacle he made. In a mile, he stood and saw the peninsula unfolding, sparkling yellow in the hot afternoon light, the emerald-green patch of the soccer field, the white tower of the chapel with its plastic Virgin in place of a bell. He heard the mob, or thought he heard the mob, but it was just the crows diving from limb to limb.

CHAPTER FIVE

THEY WERE MANY. They had crossed in canoes and skiffs and rafts, some unsafe for even a pond but somehow making the short passage, beached atop one another or tied to trees. The flat mud of Cuturú's port was punctured by their sinking feet, and the father of one of the dead teenage boys held up his son's severed, burned-looking foot with chunks of yellow stuck to the heel. Around him the mob of puertoclaveños wielded black-stained machetes, rocks, butcher knives, a few revolvers in belts, or just their bare fists, their faces sweaty, brilliant, snarled in the hot sun.

Padre Moisés cut through, excusing his way to arrive at Milton who was tied to the steel post of an unfinished streetlamp. The mob was sensual, their eyes gleaming in an outdoor discoteca atmosphere right here in the town that hated them and that they had always hated for reasons no one could remember. El Padre knew the man with the foot. They had shaken hands. There had been a baptism.

"Hola, Padre," Milton said, his face darkly netted in dried blood. He stunk of urine and something worse.

Padre Moisés put his hand on the blue harpoon tattoo, then touched the other ropes, lashed around his legs and arms and neck. He pulled on the knots and was dismayed by how taut they were, almost strangling the boy. "I'm here. Tranquilo. I won't leave you. Let me talk."

"Here is my son, Padre," said the father with the foot. His face seemed washed in blood. A bad, pink rash hooked from his collar to his eyebrows. A sexual miscue? A brush with Satan? Unshocked and weary of life, he seemed, licking at where the rash touched his mouth, digging into it with his thumb, drinking lightly from the passing bottle of rum, as if concerned by a thousand preoccupations besides Milton whose shit dripped from his shorts.

El Padre had not slept much, nor eaten anything but a plate of fried plantains they had served him at the farm. By the time he had arrived, it was only to witness the final breathing, no air for a confession, and so he prayed for the dying man's soul, and spilled some water onto his forehead. It had been a quiet death, until the end when the campesino heaved out a mixture of sounds containing God knew what story of shame he wanted understood but did not have the time for. His wife and son had already dug out a place beyond the coconut tree, adjacent to where they buried their dogs, and he would rest. Today, in this heat, the family would go to see the body, and Padre Moisés had promised to return by evening for the burial. He might not. They would wait. The body would stink through the night, and by morning a messenger would be sent. His plan, walking down the hill through the woods and across the soccer field, had been to pour a bucket of cold water onto the back of his neck and hide from the day within the cool thick walls of the chapel. He would get drunk enough to forget about the fleas. He would dream of snow.

The puertoclaveños told el Padre about the murder of their boys. He listened quietly to impossible fictions—Wilfredo was a butcher, a longtime torturer for los paracos. El Padre returned his hand to Milton's blue harpoon tattoo, his fingers dripping a steady line of sweat.

"Why not chop off his leg to start," proposed an old woman, her teeth alligatored out of her brown mouth.

The crows were up to their usual, while the buzzards, posted at the chapel tower and atop the streetlamp, coveted the foot. "Leave it for el Panguero so he knows!"

"So he knows," another said.

"You look ill, Padre," the man with the foot said, reaching out far with his tongue to itch the rash. "Come into the shadows and rest. Leave us to handle our problems."

"Listen," Padre Moisés said. "Have patience. You are a good man and I know you. You are all good people."

The morning breeze had died down, and no one could see anything straight. A snowfall would save them. El Padre had only seen snow on television, but on hot days he had a fantasy of shoving his whole head into a pile of it. Someday he would visit the mountains, when he was old, a place where things did not rot and stink the way all of Cuturú stunk now. The power was still out, the refrigerators useless.

Against Wilfredo's house, being pulled at by the women, an adolescent girl in a fluorescent green bikini staggered with her hands beneath her armpits, as if an electric current were coursing through her body. She shrieked about the pain in her chest and asked God for help. The girlfriend of the boy. She cupped her breasts with both hands and dug her knees into the mud, not crying but groaning as if her jaw were wired shut, this noise running beneath the babble of the mob.

A new bottle of rum was being passed around. El Padre reached for it, gulped, and felt dizzy, hearing boats on the river, the crows, the last breaths of the dying campesino from the night before.

"You are not a good priest," the same old woman declared, and she was probably right, he thought.

El Padre might have known better last night when he heard Wilfredo's motor. Better to have stayed up in the shade of the hills. Their farm had its own spring of cold water. Here it was boring. It was a boring time to represent a church. He should be eating snow someplace, alone or in the company of a woman like Alba. Where was she? He could sense her eyes judging him through the gaps in the wall of their house. Act, she must have been whispering. Yes, he should act. Untie Milton whose eyes were shut.

Although el Padre had arrived just three years ago and considered himself neutral, he felt closer to Cuturú and its people. He crossed to Puerto Clavel for confessions and funerals. He knew their problems. He was able to talk with the guerrillas and was safe among them, while el Suizo and Mamita would kill a priest without a second thought. He didn't understand the repulsion he felt looking at this girlfriend in the mud, this man with the rash who he remembered was a landowner, a man gifted in crop yields and in breeding pigs, one of the few making money on that side of the river during the hard years. The man's error was to openly collaborate with the guerrillas. If someone's land was being snatched by the gold companies, it was said that he went armed to protect it, that he had killed a surveyor. The foot in his hand was a warning.

A happy scream overtook the crowd as it converged around a single point. Wilfredo fought past the hands, past the father who dropped his son's foot and whacked him onto the ground with the flat of his machete. The crowd was stepping all over itself, pushing and kicking in an attempt to get Wilfredo onto the ground, but they kicked each other too and there was a bewildering moment when a few men squared off, trying to punch each other in very little space, and were separated quickly by their wives.

Even they see it, Padre Moisés thought, no one man to kill but all of us. Any object would do. It was very boring. The girlfriend hurried forward, and they held Wilfredo down so she could stomp his face with her heels. She screamed and fell backward. The women caught her. Someone grabbed el Padre's neck and screamed for the people to kill Wilfredo quick, before they regretted it.

A rope was looped around Wilfredo's neck, binding him to Milton and the post.

Wilfredo told them he was no killer.

"Shut up," Padre Moisés said, lifting himself from the hot mud, back onto his feet. "Don't speak, Wilfredo. Let me."

"Sapo de mierda," they chanted. "A killer and a snitch. Shoot him at once! De una! De una!"

"Shoot them both! De una!"

"Cut them to pieces!"

The same old woman, contorted and slippery, as if she were dripping to pieces, spat a throatful of spit onto Wilfredo's face, then launched a rock over everyone's heads. "The priest is a paramilitary," she announced, smiling. "Es un paraco de Cuturú."

"Shut up!" someone else said. "Have respect!"

"Why not take el Panguero to Bagre?" a woman suggested. "Give him to the police."

"No!" the father of the dead boy said. His rash had turned purple and seemed to be climbing up his forehead. "They'll send in a platoon to fuck our daughters."

Padre Moisés stood with his back pressed against Wilfredo's chest and had no idea what to say.

"Come into the shade, Padre." The man handed over a new bottle of rum and Padre Moisés drank. "Let us handle it."

"I'm not going to move," el Padre said.

Then, through the afternoon, nothing happened. Some retreated to the shade. Others, ashamed, paddled back across the river to milk their cows. The severed foot turned green. Someone put it into a plastic bag, but that did little good. No one had the gall to remove el Padre who, had he been a worse priest, less kind, less generous, had he taken sides in the past, would have been thrown aside.

Men pissed on the doors of nearby houses, threw their bottles onto Wilfredo's roof, and the man with the rash tied up Wilfredo's panga to his own, then kicked open his door and emerged with the impressive Yamaha, but the crowd was waiting for one man to stand up and finish the task. No one did. No one man would carry the weight for them all. They were unsure people. Nor did the cutureños come out to defend the town; even Padre Moisés looked at the shut doors, wondering about their pride.

The man with the rash approached Wilfredo and hit him over the head with the handle of the machete. Another hand gripped el Padre's one weak arm and twisted it, not hard, but enough to drop him to the ground. The man raised the blade above his head. Everyone expected Wilfredo's head would be wrenched off, that blood would jump from his neck, and, no matter how much rum they had inside them, no matter how much they had seen or how much they desired to see, they knew it would be hard to look at in the daylight.

El Padre heard a loud slapping, then another. Wilfredo's ears bled, his head was battered but unsplit, his neck bloodless in the low sun.

"You are one of them, Panguero," the man said to Wilfredo. "Don't think you are outside of it. You are leaving. I am only one father. There are others who will come. You are leaving today. You already know."

The river filled with their boats veering across the current. Some paddled with their hands, silently looking back to see Padre Moisés using his teeth and one hand to untie Wilfredo and Milton, then lead them down the street to the chapel. The eyes of the final, dejected stragglers, the old woman among them, blinked toward the road out of town and wondered at what hour the hoods appeared. Almost running them over, a narco boat of men in white shirts came speeding down the river, each boat with two outboards of seventy-five horses, packed to the brim with blue plastic barrels of coca paste. They grinned at the crappy houses of Cuturú, the plastic María in the chapel tower, the cheap canoes and cheap people in their wake.

CHAPTER SIX

AT THIRTEEN HERNÁN KNEW what went on, but Alba had stuffed his ears with cotton and held him tight against her mattress all afternoon. He heard anyway. He knew the dead boy whose foot was out there, a striker on the Puerto Clavel soccer team who had pulled a knife on the Cuturú referee when they had played a month ago. He had also thrown a rock at their boat as they passed too close to his nets, and Wilfredo said to let it go, even if Milton wanted a fight. Hernán had never met the other two, just names, campesino boys from the mountains inland, collaborators for sure, and though he easily hated the people of Puerto Clavel he was certain these boys did not deserve death.

Alba was bleeding, Hernán knew, and it was the baby rushing inside her again. When the sun hit the trees and the street turned to shadow, the man with the rash on his face slammed his heel through their door and demanded the motor.

I believe in God, Alba had said, waving a kitchen knife in front of her. Touch me, señor, and I'll kill myself.

Just the motor, the man had said, and picked it up without the cardboard for his shoulder. More men peered in and looked around for more things to take, but the man, as he kicked over their kitchen table, said, Vamos!

Kill the chickens, Alba told Hernán afterward. We'll catch the morning bus to Caucasia. She pulled out two burlap sacks and a small red suitcase she had found floating on the river.

Hernán packed the first burlap sack with his algebra textbook and notebooks, but Alba sent his books flying onto the patio. She shoved in her best pan, some bent silverware, a pair of tennis shoes, a handful of oranges, and told him to bury what they couldn't take and then deal with the chickens.

In their coop, like any river village about to be massacred, the chickens saw it coming. He snatched up the only egg and ate it raw, then knocked down Jesús the rooster with the machete and twisted his head until it broke off, sending him reeling around the orange tree. Hernán could not feel his feet. He was light-headed as he chased the hens, each with a name, and he tried to be tender, careful with their broken necks, their idiotic eyes bugging out at him as he shoved their warm bodies into the burlap sack.

"Should I clean them?" Hernán asked.

"No," Alba said, walking to the outhouse to wash herself. A circle of dried brown blood stood out on her calf.

He stuck more boards in the windows, shut off the gas to the stove, and, unable to close the valves on the water pipes to the kitchen and outhouse, broke them both with a hammer. He loaded Wilfredo's delivery cart with the two sacks and looked back inside at all they could not carry. The tank of gasoline. The dishes. The shovel, the mattresses, the sheets, the table and chairs and shelves Wilfredo had made himself. He had seen it before—their house would be gutted by their friends.

"Where is the shovel?" Alba said. She found it on her bed and jabbed the blade through the screen of the television, then kicked it off its perch. She wore her good silver earrings, simple studs Wilfredo had given her. She put a padlock on the door and paused, looking at gaps in the roof, holding her breath.

"What is it?" he said, adjusting the tennis shoes he had never worn, inherited from Milton, still too big.

"What are we forgetting?"

In the port, patterned with footprints, fruit rinds, and bottles left by the mob of puertoclaveños, the beached pangas floated a little in the river, for no one had gone out to fish or check nets or to make visits today. He looked at the gap in the sand and the bare eyelet where their panga usually rested. Dark piss stains stood out like gorges in the wood of the walls and doors of the houses. He felt his neighbors' eyes on him. Vecinos, they called themselves, with affection, even a farmer and a panguero at opposite ends of town, always vecinos, but they were not. As he and Alba walked to the plaza, he could hear their battery-powered radios and smell their food cooking. All three cantinas were closed. The grocery store and butcher shop were closed too. It was a nervous town, braced for worse. Alba never swerved in her route, seemed to care less about what she saw. She walked right through the pain, tapped her fist against the church door.

"Soy yo, Alba," she said. "Open!"

Constructed without much patience or design, of poorly mixed cement and river mud, the chapel, like a bone propped on the tip of the peninsula, leaned a little, likely to fall someday. The altar, a hull from an old panga, stood high, gold and white, as el Padre himself had painted it. Around it were small candled alcoves with hanging cutouts of the Virgin and Jesús Cristo with Lázaro risen from the dead. Padre Moisés had trimmed away the gilt borders, the numbers, the catchy publicity of the national lottery. The only other decorations were some dusty books and magazines, swollen twice their size from rain and humidity. In a corner was furniture stored for safekeeping by families who had left for good. It was a depressing church. Hernán, who prayed only when he was fishing or digging a very deep hole in the woods, made it a point to enter it as little as possible.

They found Wilfredo in a pew, eyeing the lottery posters. He looked feeble, stunned. Most of his cuts were clotting, his face pinkly marbled like a peeled guava, stitched with lines of black blood. He breathed in short little gasps and kept touching his numb teeth with his fingernails. His nose was broken and swelling up along the bottom of his eyes. Hernán heard Milton bathing just through a curtain, grunting a little so they could hear his pain too.

Alba did not rush at Wilfredo. She leaned inside one of the alcoves and crossed her chest to the dim poster of María. Wilfredo reached out to lay his hand on her belly and asked how she felt.

"I need a doctor," she said.

"How bad?"

"I don't know."

"Are we going now?" Milton asked, emerging from the bathroom in wet shorts. "I think my legs are broken."

"I have no bread," Padre Moisés said. He disappeared and came back with some dry carrots they struggled to chew.

Wilfredo grabbed Milton's head and kissed the top of it. He reached out for Hernán who stood stiffly, looking at the door, and then pulled him onto his lap, though he was too big for it. "Drink water. We'll walk to the highway and then you can rest. Did you see anyone?"

"The town seems empty," Alba said. "I don't know. The whole plaza is closed."

"We'll take the trail," Wilfredo said. "We have to avoid the road."

Outside, Wilfredo slammed his fist against the door of the grocery store and then broke the only window with a rock. No one opened. He insulted the owner's name, so the whole town could hear. At this, Hernán felt sharp pins in his head, his throat dry. He imagined the owner opening the door and shooting his father in the face. Padre Moisés shuffled his feet and promised he would collect the money owed for past deliveries and send it. He said good-bye.

He had to walk upriver to a funeral.

As the family turned down a side street at the edge of town, the houses lit up, as did the two streetlamps, the chapel, every single television suddenly at top volume. People swore and opened their doors to see if it was true and saw Wilfredo and his family. He looked away from them, hurrying into the darkness of the soccer field, through the goal posts, which Hernán touched for good luck, and then took them up one of the numerous paths into the woods. At the top of the first hill, they looked down at the yellow lights along the river, a black line of water, and downriver more lights.

The path was wide enough for two people to walk side by side, and it was sunken to a wet ditch by so many feet, twisting up into the tiny farming villages. Mosquitoes hovered over Alba who wrapped up her face in a newly sewn yellow bandana and covered her feet and legs with fresh mud. They moved slowly, stopping at the tops of hills so Milton and Wilfredo could switch the sacks from one shoulder to another. Hernán, the red suitcase in one hand, reached out to feel the prickly plants and the dark spaces of the woods. His feet, wet now from a puddle, slid back and forth with every step in the big shoes.

"My legs," Milton whispered, every so often. "Dios mío."

"What's wrong?" Hernán asked.

"I don't know."

"Let me carry your sack."

"No."

When they neared the perimeter of the hacienda full of indios, Wilfredo led them off the trail and into the dark of the woods, pulling back branches, trying to make a steady path to the road. They got turned around. Wilfredo looked at the sky for a sign of direction but was stumped by it. Hernán prayed, promising to be generous to the new baby when it was born.

"Mierda," Hernán said, hugging the little red suitcase to his chest.

"What happened?" Milton said, looking down at the old tennis shoes on his brother's feet.

"I forgot something."

"Shut up," Wilfredo said. "I hear the road. I think."

In a shoebox, hidden beneath the roof of the outhouse, Hernán had stored his findings from digs in the woods and abandoned houses. They were little things, but he kept them neat, clean, and in order. He had a couple long AK-47 bullets, fishhooks, an unused syringe with malaria vaccine, an owl skull, a long piece of snake skin, a green feather from someone's parrot, an unsmoked cigar, an un-cracked handheld mirror. He turned away but could not see any trail now. There was no way back to Cuturú. He would call el Padre and tell him to bury the shoebox somewhere, but could he trust him?

"Walk," Milton said. "Stop crying."

"I'm not crying."

After an hour, without a gap in the canopy of the trees, when the burlap sacks were catching, tearing on the brittle dead trees of the marsh, their feet soaked and raw within their shoes, Hernán felt the hard-packed gravel under his feet. They pushed north along the edge of the road until they came to a ravine, slipped back into the trees, and lay down as a truck roared past. They covered Alba entirely with a blanket so the mosquitoes could not bite her.

"Are they coming for us?" Alba said, grabbing her head, then reaching up with no purpose into the air and grabbing at nothing.

CHAPTER SEVEN

TWO SHARP LIGHTS BROKE through the morning fog. The bus had no windows, no real walls, just gaps at the end of each row of wooden bench seats, while the sides were expanded with iron supports to hold an oversized roof, piled to the sky with sacks of produce, chickens, a young pig, chairs, a mattress. It seemed more like a carnival float than a bus. They called them chivas, and if you had no boat and could not afford the taxis, this was your option. All the mud and dust could not conceal the vivid yellow and red and blue paint, and on its rear was a depiction of the Virgin, who looked like a blue-eyed prostitute dressed in leather, beside the soiled and dented face of a monstrous Jesús Cristo.

No one seemed surprised to see the family with two sacks and a red suitcase standing there in the middle of nowhere. The passengers were mostly farmers from the hills, a few in creased, unworn city clothes, having just visited their home villages, and though a couple knew Wilfredo or at least recognized him from the river, they were respectful enough to look away from his face, which seemed chewed on by dogs and bloated by a drowning. The panga was gone or the motor broken, they figured: no one rode in a chiva for fun.

The driver climbed onto the roof, shifting around baggage, kicking the pig out of his way, and pulling back a thick black tarp. Wilfredo passed up the sacks. Milton stepped forward with the red suitcase, and was embarrassed before the men of the bus as he could hardly lift it over his head.

Alba had climbed the stairs and was leaning over the side of a bench seat, waiting for someone to notice her belly and give up a spot. It was a curse to live so far from the city, and so the riders, milking their one advantage of a seat, a pleasant view of the countryside, were hesitant to give in. Hernán tried to brace his hands against Alba's waist, as the bus jerked forward with a harsh shifting of gears. Wilfredo crouched on the edge, staring at the woods as the road curved around the flooded marshes of el río Puerco, eventually distancing itself from the basin, entering the hills where windfalls sent the bus at right-angled detours into the woods, and, at one point the road dropped away entirely into an abyss. Besides Alba, all the passengers were forced to descend and walk to the other side, while la chiva gained enough speed to get across. Here, a young campesino saved his honor by leaving his seat to Alba.

The road was badly maintained, but the thick tires did not pop as the bus jumped over rocks and divots, constantly shaking out of or into a higher gear. A vulture swooped down onto the roof for a moment and skimmed across the road, too heavy to fly much. Hernán watched the birds until his eyes shut, la chiva's engine louder as it accelerated, yet, always, just as it reached top speed, the brakes would screech and somehow more passengers would pinch into the aisles, the lithe driver again on the roof to create space for baggage.

An hour passed. At every stop, Hernán felt they were being thrust into boiling water. Campesinos hung out the doors, both hands clenched around metal bars, nonchalant, gazing vaguely at the sliding green hills, liquid in the heat. Beyond Turbai nothing at all was familiar to Hernán. The landmarks of Cuturú, the holes dug and pending digging, the various pools where he had tried to catch trout and where there would always be trout, the shade of the acacia tree where Milton said he took off Lucila's pink underwear

36

and put his fingers into her to know if she smelled good, were lost. A bright weed of foam hung at the corner of Alba's mouth, the bandana knotted over her eyes, and Hernán prayed for her safety, not the baby's. He fell into brief, deep slumbers, despite the bumps, and was slammed awake by a woman's hip mashing down on his head as the bus lurched up over the lip of paved road to Caucasia.

"Two hours," a woman said.

They passed by a small town with the broad thatched roof of a restaurant and an immense smoking grill. They paused to load a passenger, and a silver Toyota Tacoma pulled up beside them. Milton lay flat on the floor and an old woman with deformed hands, knowing, shrouded his entire body within the billows of her skirt. In the back of the truck rode shirtless paramilitaries, strangely pale with shaved heads and AK-47s in their laps. They examined the rows, not looking for anyone special, but how could you ever know?

Wilfredo's face was bleeding; he had scratched at the cuts. He did not bow his head or hide his face, but said to Milton, "Get up," as the chiva left town.

"Wilfredo," Alba said. "Mi amor! I have contractions."

"She's hemorrhaging," a woman said. "Stop the bus."

"No, continue!" another barked at the driver. "Al hospital! Chofér, apúrese! La señora is giving birth."

Alba sprawled across the bench seat, and women from different ends of la chiva formed a circle around her, fanning her face with a straw hat, spilling rum into her mouth, saying that they knew her pain and lying about the distance. "Only a half hour to Caucasia," they said. "Hurry, chofér. Don't stop."

The driver, who seemed to enjoy the challenge, ignored potential passengers with their arms raised at different crossroads. They passed ranches, big white-and-black herds of beef cattle wagging their tails at the flies as they grazed. At one farm, cows were being herded with sticks toward an auction ring, big pickup trucks lining the drive, men in cowboy hats shaking hands and speaking on cell phones.

Hernán had been shoved in between Milton and another man at the rear of the bus. He was unsure about this kindness from the passengers, these men in cleaned-up white shirts for church, one from the city telling him it would be fine, that the doctors had recently sewn up Reynaldo Vidal, the bullfighter who was gored by a bull just last month, losing two liters of blood. He was already walking around and giving interviews on television.

They passed numerous churches, and the passengers crossed their chests at the sight of each. They passed the military barracks, the bullring, and finally clanked up onto the long iron bridge over el río Cauca, a brown, foamy vein carrying south the waters of inferior rivers. A little panga sped by full of red sacks. If you went back down it, Hernán thought, you could find your way to Cuturú, keeping to the right side at every channel, watching for the shoals of Bledo, going north against the current until you reached the confluence where you better have enough gas to get up it. In these connections of water, these embattled currents to nowhere villages, Alba had lost the other two babies.

La chiva, its horn bellowing the emergency, was too wide for Caucasia's crowded streets. It wobbled through traffic, past la plaza de Bolívar and the central market and lines of people waving merchandise at the bus, past a stubborn old man pushing a cart full of papayas, and finally to the hospital, a low colorless building with a rusted-out arch across the half-moon entrance. La chiva would not fit. They stopped in the middle of traffic and, no time for a stretcher, Wilfredo carried Alba, while a kind woman from the bus supported her legs.

Hernán and Milton waited for the driver to pass down their burlap sacks and red suitcase. The pig had dug through the baggage and eaten one of the hens. The campesino apologized frantically to them and to others who had lost things, who were pushing him around and pointing fingers at his chest. They demanded their money back, and the driver refused. Police arrived, unwilling to side with anyone, ordering the driver to move his chiva immediately from the road. One passenger insulted the policeman who raised his stick and asked him to say it again. He did not, so in a tide of horns and blue diesel smoke, la chiva disappeared into the city. Hernán crossed his chest at the image of the muddy Virgin.

CHAPTER EIGHT

JAMMED INTO THE HALLWAY of the hospital, Alba opened her eyes to a hot beam of sun on her body. On the back of her tongue was the rancid taste of raw onions, and a bag of scarlet blood drained down into her hand. She touched her belly and felt the gauze diaper and dressings, a semi-distant, medicated pain in her pelvis. She clawed at the mosquito bites on her face until they bled, and she cried for a while. Nurses in white streaked by but none tended to her. Who fed me the onions? she wanted to ask, wishing for a toothbrush or a glass of juice. She slept again and woke in a small room with cracked green plaster peeling off the ceiling and a single triangular window covered by a thin green curtain. Four other women shared this space, each in a corner, grinning tiredly at the ceiling or sleeping. Alba lay in the very center. Where are the nurses? she wanted to ask the young mothers. Where is Wilfredo? She rubbed her feet together against the cotton sheets and felt the dry river mud from home. Her hair seemed greased through, solid as a pile of wool. Had Hernán cleaned the hens yet, or were they rotting in the burlap sacks? She slept again, awoke to see that the bag of blood was gone, her wrist bandaged. Her sister Lidia's voice talked to her now—in the remote static of last month's telephone call—about how they were welcome in Bogotá, far away from heat and headless teenagers, palms and blighted banana trees. Bogotá was a mountain of concrete and electric light, a brick house with two stories and a

40

bathtub, and two happy nieces riding speedy buses through avenues of towering buildings. The weight of it paralyzed her. She would never understand a place that large.

She opened her eyes to Wilfredo's brother Tuts, his sucked-in feminine cheeks and big ears full of gray hair and sawdust—no wife to make him bathe, either gay or just in love with his tools, good boards, and nails.

"I'm sorry, Albita," Tuts said. He kissed her cheek with papery lips. "You've been attacked by mosquitoes, mi amor. I had to lend you some blood. I've got the rare type."

Hernán was caressing her feet, and Wilfredo stood at the side of the bed and touched the bracelet on her arm, which she imagined said *Mother of the dead baby*. It was vexing to be touched in this way, and where were the nurses and the doctor with his sure voice, a man in a tie asking her to sign her name?

"Where is Milton?" she said.

"He's at my shop," Tuts said. "His legs don't work."

"Legs?"

"How do you feel?" Hernán said.

"Horrible, mi amor," she said, "but it's good to see you."

"We have to go soon," Wilfredo said. His face had become a map of the countryside, swollen here with blue hills, unclean and patterned with yellow pus rivers and dark-brown trails of blood. His nose was crooked and smashed, a leachy black gash on his forehead, the mark of a machete or rock. "We can't afford for you to stay."

"I made a comfortable bed for you, Albita," Tuts said, "and I'll keep the saws quiet for a couple days."

"How much is it?" she said. "I still haven't seen the doctor."

"He saw you," Tuts said. "He was no shaman, just a typical youngster with a bad face."

"He saved you," Hernán said.

"I need to see him," Alba said. "I have questions. How much?"

She looked at Wilfredo and sat up on her elbows. "Did you pay for this kind of service?"

"Tranquila, mamá," Hernán said.

He grabbed her dirty foot and squeezed it.

"Vamos, Hernáncito," Tuts said and pulled a curtain all around the bed, stepping out to be among the happy mothers. Before she was ready, Wilfredo lifted off her gown and pulled over her yellow dress with red palms, which smelled of diesel and dust and the sweet antiseptic and blood from her dressings. He slid her sandals onto her feet and then handed her a large pair of blue underwear she had never seen.

"Where are my earrings?" she said, pinching her bare earlobes.

"I'll get you new ones," he said.

"How much?" she said. "All of it?"

"I talked to Lidia already. She'll send the money tomorrow. We have to leave soon."

"Will you ask them for my earrings?"

"It's no use."

She sat up and looked at her feet. "Can you at least get a nurse?"

"I'll try."

"Por favor."

Before he could step out from the curtain she grabbed his hand. He pressed his raw face against her neck. Wait, she wanted to say. Wait. No hurry now inside the curtains. Tuts and Hernán will get it. Tell them we are planning for Bogotá. Please. But he was pulling her up and to the floor where the other mothers would see her.

CHAPTER NINE

AT FIRST, TUTS'S WOOD SHOP had never been so silent. The men, including Milton, drank cold beer most of the hot afternoon, while Alba tried to sleep on a mattress covered in sawdust and stained with machine oil. Hernán pounded some boards together, wandered around the unfinished neighborhood, did some halfhearted digging for guaca and found nothing. On the morning of the second day, they picked up the baby from the hospital. They buried it in one of Hernán's holes, marking the spot with a wood cross Tuts had varnished and carved up with the name, Patricio Rodríguez, the date of birth and death, and a simple message: *Dios lo llamó.* God called him.

"I have to work now," Tuts said, after the prayer was done and the hole was sealed.

The following afternoon, beef cows watched as Wilfredo and Alba hobbled uphill into Tuts's wood shack. The saws went quiet, and in a few minutes they emerged in different clothes with the two burlap sacks and the red suitcase, followed by Hernán and Milton. A yellow taxi came up the hill past a big blue swimming pool, the driver looking at the unfinished houses, the dead banana trees, a large herd of black cattle wandering through severed barbed wire, a bulldozer digging out a massive hole for a hotel. Seeing Tuts waving in the window and the family on the stoop, the driver brought his taxi to a halt.

The bus terminal was busy in the evening. A day's worth of people were sweating out their departures and arrivals and farewells, catching one last whiff of the fishy odor of the nearby río Cauca, pink in the twilight.

At the side of a blue-striped bus with a sign saying EXPRESO A MEDELLÍN-BOGOTÁ, Hernán watched the loading of the burlap sacks and saw his underwear in the gaps of the netting. He looked as if he had been riding in the bow of the panga for a long time and had just jumped out on firm land. He was dressed for the capital, even if it was twenty-four hours away, wearing his new white cotton socks, the gray tennis shoes too large for his feet, and stiff black jeans cinched to his waist with a leather shoelace.

Tuts did not meet their eyes. He mumbled about the time and stopped short on normal words, repeating that it was a shame to go anywhere in a hurry. He filled the gap of a missing tooth with his tongue. He measured the size of the cramped terminal the same as wood for hotel beds or chairs, and said, "The design is faulty. I've heard the same is true of Bogotá, in general, but how can I know?"

"If you don't know something, just shut your mouth," Milton said because he was staying behind with Tuts to learn a trade and because his aunt Lidia's husband Ramón had made it understood that four was too many in his house. Milton smoked carefully, leaned against a bus soon departing to Cartagena, and said to Hernán, "Stay close to Ramón. Papá will be as lost as—" but he was interrupted by Alba hugging him and kissing his chin and mouth.

"Vamos!" the driver of the express said.

"Adiós," Tuts called. "Good luck."

"Adiós," Wilfredo said.

"Adiós," Hernán said.

Wilfredo pushed Hernán down the aisle of blue padded seats and blue curtains on tinted windows, and into the back row so they could see who boarded. The bus was empty but for a pale man with bright red thighs in brown Bermudas, who sat near the front and talked to himself in a monotone drawl. "Buenas noches," he said to Alba.

Even before they reached the city limits, past the tar and creosote fumes of the factories, the driver was gunning the motor, swerving around horse carts and bicycles and taxis, catcalling pretty girls, honking and cussing out the window at slow drivers. The road alternated between pavement and dirt, followed close along the western bank of el río Cauca, the towns nothing but huts on stilts, crowded with barefoot children who waved. They could hear the express miles away. Men looked up from their seats in the doorways. The bus was a symbol of the modern era, but if no one raised an arm for it to stop, it passed in a flash, the narrow road clearing of dogs, goats, and horses, while the driver hung out the window yelling: "A Medellín, a Medellín! A Bogotá, a Bogotá!"

Then the river was gone. The road curled its way up a sudden rise into the woods, the vegetation thinning out to long stretches of pasture.

Wilfredo leaned across a half-asleep Alba and pressed his forehead against the window. The saws had unnerved him. Their grinding sent him walking downhill and into Caucasia where he sat by the river and watched the pangas go by, guessing at the weight and route of their freight.

It was not safe, Tuts told him, to show himself alive on those streets, especially by the port, but who could blame him for saying good-bye to it? He imagined his panga moored at the river's edge in Puerto Clavel and some other panguero using it improperly. He hoped the motor died for good.

"Are your ears still ringing from the saws?" Alba said.

"Yes."

"We'll come back."

"For what?" he said, but knew she was right.

Alba felt cold in the heat, her eyes the yellow of chicken fat. She wore a white turtleneck with a coffee stain on the left breast. She was not ready. She bled still. She had hardly spoken during the days in Caucasia. Every subject seemed taboo and every thought seemed like a great weight to lug out into the air of conversation, and she was weak in the frenzy of Tuts's house that was not a house but a workroom with nowhere to sit or talk or think. But she would mourn later for the baby, when there was time; she was more worried about her sister Lidia, the great exaggerator of the family. Her husband Ramón drank with anxiety and often boxed her into the corners of the house. Once, after a fight, she fled to Cuturú, staying a week, on the first day excited, smelling everything, bathing in the river, dancing with men she had known since childhood, who saw her black eyes and were gracious to her. On the third day she got bored. She complained about the heat, could not sleep the siesta, and watched a coca farmer get whipped by el Suizo for not paying tax on the crop he moved. On the fourth day Ramón called and said he was coming for her. This proved his love. He told her all about the improvements he was making to their house—a tub, an oven, a second-floor bedroom, a terrace—a house so big there was no room for Milton. Ramón? Alba closed her eyes and saw his bright-blue denim shirt, the half-moon links of the silver bracelet. Like all short men, he was too close to the ground to be confident. He owned a tailor shop in Bogotá, and likely his success was overstated like that of all the cutureños who came home well dressed, bought everyone rum at la cantina, and then had to borrow bus fare back to the city.

In Tarazá, even at this hour, the bus began to fill. Some had potato sacks or dingy cotton pillowcases, while others sported black suitcases on wheels. They found seats and instantly fell asleep.

Hernán awoke to the pale-faced rider with the red thighs across the aisle from him, muttering about the time, the lack of speed, the price of travel. Morning, and all of Medellín was in his window, the bright glass, the white elevated train, and the green walls of mountain on all sides. At the terminal passengers had descended, and new ones took their seats. They were lighter skinned, a head taller than the country people. More clogged up the aisles as the bus began the long ascent into the mountains. Towns up here were quick pieces of white brick and white crosses on ledges where people had died, the rivers no longer muddy but green in the rising sun. In some places, sandbags were piled high around white huts with zigzag lines of orange cones and a soldier raising his hand to halt the bus. The soldiers were young with serious acne and lethargic faces, staring at the passengers and asking who was who and where from, and then waving for a complete unloading.

While Wilfredo handed over his ID and answered questions about his origins, his destination, a soldier gave Hernán a colorful flyer with a photograph of an ex-guerrilla in new civilian clothes. The man was decorating a Christmas tree with a little girl, and a lightbulb flashed beside his head. *Guerrillero! Demobilize. Bring us your arms and explosives to receive a reward. We respect life and liberty. Don't hesitate any longer and do it now! Call toll free: 146. Any authority, division of the military or police, will receive you.*

Hernán folded the paper and put it in his pocket. Other passengers let theirs drop to the floor. The army was engaged in an unsettling campaign of friendliness and positive thinking about the security of the country; a soldier boarded to wish everyone a safe and pleasurable trip, and on the way out of town, a dozen soldiers guarding a bridge gave them the thumbs-up gesture.

In Santuario, two hours west of Medellín, there were yellow signs forewarning a confrontation and ordering the bus to turn back. The passengers slouched in their seats, hearing the shrill crack of automatic rifles, the low boom of a gas explosion. The driver ignored the sign, turning sharply onto a dirt road, and they cut across an open ridge of lime trees and a fenced-in estate.

"A dead man!" yelled a woman in a white straw hat. "What a shame!"

Hernán looked out at a soldier, his legs frozen in a twisted dancing pose beside a piece of bloody grass, not the first corpse he had seen. He searched for an orange in Alba's bag, licked the cool sticky skin and tasted the dirt of their patio. Her fingers moved stiffly through his hair, sliding down the neck of his shirt, scratching his spine, until Wilfredo pushed her down and draped his body over them. Others were ducking too, waiting for the shatter, the flat tire, the sudden scream that would mean they were in cross fire. An old lady pulled out religious cards with the Virgin on them and prayed aloud. The passengers with the nicer luggage lay on the floor and screamed for the driver to go faster. They passed a group of guerrilleros on horseback and in a few minutes hit the open road.

A few passengers applauded, while another woman yelled, "We should have turned back. You put us all at risk."

"Shut your fucking mouth," the driver said without heat or disrespect.

"Are you frightened?" Alba said.

"Yes," Hernán said.

"Strange," the pale-faced man next to Hernán said. "I came through two days ago, and it was peaceful."

Pine trees bent past. Down from the highlands and into the valley of el río Magdalena, the express made better time. The passengers pushed the windows open as far as they would go and tied up the blue curtains to let in the hot wind of swamp. In Honda, the streets swarmed with vendors, with sweaty eyebrows and black roasted corn, blood sausage, tall cups of mango, pink papaya with cheese. The heat was unbearable. At six o'clock, the national anthem played as it did every day on every radio station.

"Vamos," the passengers yelled. "What express! This is not a serious company."

"A bunch of thieves!" the woman in the straw hat said.

The pale-faced man rubbed minty ointment into his burned thighs and said, "Get ready, muchacho, this last climb is going to do away with our patience."

This road was never straight. It curved so sharply that some of the semitrucks had to almost stop to make their turns. The driver gunned the motor in low gears, swerving for a glimpse of the oncoming traffic, seeing nothing—the passengers leaning too—and on good faith, or no faith, just craziness, made a move to pass two trucks at once, faced with the lights of an oncoming semi or car with its horn blaring. They swerved quickly ahead into the right lane or braked hard back to their original spot. The passengers were too tired, too afraid to protest. They seemed to have entered the clouds. The crisp tropical light faded and was replaced by fog, then rain, and the road was slick black.

"Don't worry. The driver's accustomed to this," the pale man said, as Hernán flinched at a close call. "Slower might be even more dangerous."

Past thousands of greenhouses, they kept loading up the aisle of the express, risking mutiny from the passengers who did not sleep but sat bolt upright in their seats as they reached the city. All the dark-green trees turned to concrete sidewalks and iron scaffolding and redbrick. A dark shade had been thrown over the world. There was no grand entrance, no gates or flags. Just superstores with white searchlights weaving through the sky, and neon-yellow, blue, and red signs across the roofs—ÉXITO, HOMECENTER, CARREFOUR. Through the bright windows rich city people swam confidently through the colorful aisles of products.

"This must be it," Wilfredo said as they crossed la avenida las Américas.

It was nothing, no terminal, just a busy intersection where half the passengers stepped off to hail other buses. Hernán pushed up against them with the red suitcase and decided he would copy everything they did. "Vamos," he said to his parents who had faces of the type of people who would sit on the bus till the end of the road and the driver kicked them off.

PART II

The Capital

CHAPTER TEN

HERNÁN AND WILFREDO SQUINTED through rain at the lit boards in the front windows of city buses, looking for the words *Tres Esquinas*. Rain steadily soaked their clothes, as the sound of a hundred tires tearing through water ate at their nerves. Safe, dry, blue, and warm, it seemed a mistake to get off the express. They were alone. No river. Wilfredo was clueless.

"What's going on?" Alba said.

Hernán read every word on every sign and pointed at one, approaching, passing. "Tres Esquinas," he said. "Mierda! There comes another!"

They set their baggage in the doorway and pushed past bony knees to the back row of seats packed with wind-burned people who smelled like wet wool and wood smoke. As they headed southward, the highway grew dimmer and narrower, and the skyscrapers and shopping centers turned into auto shops, factories, brick tenements, warehouses. The bus slowed at red lights and ran through them, swerving sharply for potholes, missing pieces of the dislodged road, and stopping suddenly in the dark for a lone passenger.

"We left the city," Hernán said, as they entered the darker hills.

"Let's trust in Lidia," Alba said. "She said, 'Tres Esquinas.' There can't be more than one."

"You are on the right bus," said a tall kid with a scarf over his face.

"Gracias!" Alba said.

The pavement terminated at the top of a ridge within a narrowing alley of closed produce stands. Hernán helped Alba down, while Wilfredo picked up their luggage. It was a sloping marketplace of cantinas and shops. At the highest point stood an antenna with red lights, and in every direction spread the imperfect lines of yellow and white lights over the hills of the slum.

Two soldiers in camouflage rain gear and neon-orange vests, their rifles hanging across their stomachs, stood under the awning of a grocery where Alba called her sister and yelled, as if to launch her voice across the silent expanse of the neighborhood, "We arrived! Come get us!"

After a long wait, Ramón appeared in the dark night, stepping around puddles, and without a glance for the soldiers or anyone he went straight to Alba in whom he recognized the figure of his own wife. He embraced her and kissed her cheek. He picked up the two sacks and said, "Entonces qué? Follow me. You were expecting Bogotá?" He nodded at this secondary city. "This is Cazucá. It's new."

Ramón walked fast and gave no tour. He did not ask how the ride had been or about Milton. Nor did he praise their skill for navigating the dark city, failing to see the miracle of this encounter. They had expected a hunched, soft-tongued, weary-eyed tailor. A servant. But he walked like he owned the street, like the rain was no bother. His mind seemed to have recorded each puddle, rise, or dip, while in short time their feet were wet and caked, their nerves tight from the echoing noises of barking and a man screaming at someone.

Streetlamps gave shape to wider paths but also concealed, along with the rain, the quality of the houses. Lights marked some doorways and made clean straight rows up over a ridge and down into a zigzagging maze of ravines with a dark hump of earth at the center.

"Where are the people?" Hernán said.

"Afraid in their beds," Ramón said. "There's a cleaning going on. Careful here. Puddles."

They followed him past the open doors of a billiard hall where men scoped shots with worn cues, always facing the street. Cleaning, Ramón explained in a lowered voice, was killing to keep the neighborhood decent. A little controversial, he said, whether it worked or not.

Turning up a steep alley, Hernán stopped to let Alba catch up. He breathed hard in the thin mountain air, but after twenty hours on the bus it felt good to determine the direction of his body. They stopped at a high structure pasted together with drippy cement. Ramón rattled open a blue metal door.

Lidia was waiting there in the threshold, and as soon as she saw Alba's sick face, she dragged her upstairs to the bedroom. It was shocking to hear Alba so awake suddenly and without breath to say all she had brought inside her. She complained about the long ride, Tuts with his horrible saws, the lost panga, the ingrates of Cuturú—God would pay them back.

"Ramón!" Lidia yelled from the top of the stairs.

"Yes, my love?"

"Bring Alba a cup of aguapanela with lime and honey! She's sick!"

"Listo, mi amor."

Hernán's cousins were small, improved replicas of their mother, their eyes black in cheap blue makeup. Caterín kissed him gently and fully on the cheek, while Marta's kiss hit hard and dry below his ear. Marta, who was his age, critically peeled an orange seed from his collar. She seemed to calculate his height, weight, intelligence, and decided he amounted to very little. She was quick-eyed, touchy, looking at everything around her as if it were a tiring question only she could answer.

"Come sit with us," the older Caterín said, a silver stud bobbing at the center of her tongue. She was beautiful with a thick boyish body but not fat, her clothes extremely tight so that flesh puffed out against the seams. Her eyebrows had been razored off and painted back on with a more drastic arch.

He followed them into the TV darkness of the living room, where half the floor was covered in red mosaic tiles, the rest bare cement. He sat down on a sagging couch beside Marta. On TV was a show about a fake priest who meddled in everyone's business and fell in love with a beautiful blonde black woman who wore a chinchilla fur on her neck. The screen jittered into white flashes every so often. They would take turns standing up to whack the side of the box.

"How is Milton?" Caterín said.

"He hurt his legs, but he's fine," Hernán said. "He's going to study carpentry."

"Hah," Marta said. She put her elbows on her knees the way a boy would and flexed her arms, grimacing as her whole body tensed up. "Carpentry? I don't believe it. How many tattoos does he have?"

"He has just the harpoon."

"Look." Marta wrenched up the leg of Caterín's tight blue jeans to unveil a black, cheaply sketched hourglass at its midpoint. Above it, a finger curled around a dagger.

"What does it mean?" he said.

"Time," Caterín said. "I'm already sick of it."

"What?" Marta said. "You told me you loved it."

"Our luck was bad," said Hernán before he realized he was speaking. "I was going to leave Cuturú to study in any case, but I left early. We all left."

"You're cute," Marta said. "You don't have fleas, do you?" She shoved her head into the couch cushion and laughed. Hernán had played with her twice in Cuturú but those times on the river, pretending he could swim in a safe yellow pool, were useless now. Born in Caucasia, the girls had become rolas, cachacas, mountain girls, bogotanas of pale faces and cold hands.

"You should know this, primo," Marta said. "I get tired of the newcomers and their sad stories. All they do is lie." Spheres of TV flashed across her eyes. "Like the señor who told me that a paramilitary raped his wife and then him. Can you believe that? How long will you stay? Eh? I liked this neighborhood empty and quiet."

Caterín smacked the stud against her teeth and removed her socks to examine the bottoms of her toes. "It's probably true. Men rape men. I've heard it."

"You barely even talk," Marta said, poking Hernán's shoulder with her thumb. "Hola?"

"I'm so tired," he said. "It was a stressful trip."

"He sounds like an adult," Marta said. "You are not on vacation."

"Shut up," Caterín said, rubbing off little rolls of dirt from between her toes and sniffing them, "or you'll get slapped."

"By who?"

Caterín raised her hand high into the air, flinging back the lids on her big intelligent eyes, Marta flinching, and then they all laughed, Hernán laughing so hard—desperately—that Marta grabbed his ear, and told him to slow down.

CHAPTER ELEVEN

IT WAS A STRUGGLE to stay awake that first night, but Hernán wanted to know where and when everyone fell asleep. Alba sprawled across the big bed upstairs with Lidia, Wilfredo wrapped in jackets on the sofa by the television, Ramón at the kitchen table drinking on his own, mumbling, pleased he had convinced Wilfredo not to go find work at the market on his first day. Ramón clicked shut the green metal doors that kept them safe, one to the roof, the terraza, the other onto the street. In and out all night, Ramón fell asleep somewhere unknown. The little bedroom had a wide open door to the living room. Hernán shared a bed with Marta, a temporary thing, divided with a red curtain from Caterín's bed. He could hear Caterín's moans in her sleep, as if she had a stomachache, and Marta seemed tortured by some open-eyed attack, continuously rolling over to push him off the edge—"I'm going crazy," she whispered. "Sleep, and don't look at me." It was a cold night when you stopped moving, and Marta made it clear they could not touch bodies at all.

When Hernán awoke the next morning, the girls were gone. A woman was shrieking, "Malo, malo, malo, cochino, cochino de mierda!" through the cool wall, and he heard a howling child being slapped.

Ramón was gone. Lidia was gone. Wilfredo sat awake on the sofa with someone's hat over his eyes. Hernán went upstairs to find Alba buried in wool blankets. He kissed her hair full of little white specks of scalp and looked inside the pink holes in her earlobes without her earrings. Up here were no tiles yet, just a trail of jaggedly cut red carpet around the bed, a poster picture of Jesús Cristo with bloody thorns in his head. A clock beside the bed said 11 A.M. and in all the dim drainage of light through the windows the objects were secret.

"I'll be up soon," Alba said.

"Are you sick?" he said.

"Yes."

Downstairs, he turned the knobs on the stove and smelled the gas, the same stuff of Cuturú. He boiled water, cleaned and loaded the coffee filter himself, the same brown sock they used at home. He put too much in, but better too much always. There were eggs in a basket. He put oil in a pan, crookedly diced onion and a too-juicy tomato. He was slow and clumsy but he knew how, and he fried it all, cracking the eggs on the edge of the counter, beating them in with a wooden spoon as long as his arm.

"Don't forget the salt," Wilfredo said, rubbing his eyes in the doorway.

"It's eleven o'clock in the morning," Hernán said. "We slept forever."

They sat together on the sofa with plastic plates on their knees, eating with urgency, glancing up occasionally at the empty black screen of the television. No bread, so with saltine crackers they scooped up yellow specks of egg, orange oil, and tomato juice.

Wilfredo said, "Stay here with your mother. I'm going to the corner to get Alba something for her sickness. Her cousin has a store there."

"He's from the river," Hernán said.

"If anyone knocks, don't answer. Make eggs for Alba too."

Hernán flipped the television switch on and off. He picked up the heavy red telephone and listened to the dial tone. Who would he call? He made himself a third egg, then made eggs for Alba who let them go cold on the bed stand and sent him back downstairs. She said even the sight of him hurt her eyes.

"I could read to you," he said.

"I'll be up soon," she said. "Be good."

He looked at the food in the full refrigerator, carrots, cabbages, corn, and a porous block of stinky campesino cheese that he shaved off with a spoon in little ribbons he sucked the juice from and chewed up slowly. He tried mustard for the first time, spread it with a spoon on saltines. "What a salsa," he said. He found paper and wrote his name on it. He drew a picture of a dinosaur, not so good. He painstakingly made each of the girls' beds and looked at their underwear, held it up in the light, pink and white, imagining Caterín's breasts, which he hoped to see at some point.

He was not bored. He heard voices and barking on the street, the grinding of engines and screeching air brakes of the buses, occasionally a catcall, an insult, a question. He put it all together and decided it was a normal neighborhood, just crowded.

When the girls came home he was pretending to complete the living room floor with the red mosaic tiles. They wore pleated blue flannel skirts, white socks, and blue V-neck sweaters with the stitched name of their school. The perfect arches of Caterín's fake eyebrows gleamed as she clicked beats of a song with her silver stud against her teeth. Marta checked their room to see if he'd snooped.

"Alba made the beds. She must be better," Marta said. "You smell like sweat. You know you can use our bathtub."

"I was cooking," he said.

"No school tomorrow," Marta said. "Thank God for holidays and our school is hard. You can't afford it, I bet, not yet. It costs half of mamá's salary."

Marta said she was too tired to play any games, so Hernán saw nothing of the neighborhood that day. That was fine. They watched the same TV shows he knew in Cuturú, and if it weren't for the cold, the smell of shit in the plumbing, he could be there. Wilfredo came in drunk. He sat on the sofa, rubbing his eyes without reacting to the TV jokes, and he fell asleep with his head against the wall.

"Do you like our house?" Marta said.

"I like it," Hernán said.

"It's big," she said, "and it won't fall. I am not in love with anyone, but Cate is in love with Antonio. The problem is he lies to her."

"Shut up," Caterín said. She was writing English words—*apple, car, dog*—in long columns on a sheet of paper, a pink sucker in her cheek.

"We don't know anything yet," Hernán said. "We have to establish ourselves."

"What is he talking about?" Marta said.

"He's fine," Caterín mumbled.

"Who's fine?" Ramón said, leaning in the doorway with a bag of chicken parts. Today he looked like a tailor in a collared blue shirt and tie. "And you, Wilfredo, wake up! Tomorrow we leave at dawn. You'll see the biggest market in the country. Hernán, you think I forgot you? Here. I made you a uniform."

"What?" Marta said. "Is he going to our school? My God."

CHAPTER TWELVE

THEY MOVED IN THE OPPOSITE DIRECTION of Tres Esquinas, of what he knew. They crossed foul drainages and slipped down muddy ledges between clusters of houses, cautious at the corners of eye-level roofs, the path twisting into a wider road, then a path again. Dogs tested their chains. Someone's tank was losing water. A nearby TV spoke of war in Iraq. Little progress was made here in Wilfredo's knowledge of the landscape, in the predawn darkness. Occasionally, they fell into step with other men, hooded with scarves over their mouths, a woman dragging an empty wheelbarrow, her head wrapped up in the legs of a pair of jeans. The path turned to pavement, the streetlamps brighter, no longer of varied wood or wire but solid steel, and down one more slope the road leveled out among closed shops and brick tenements.

The golden current of la Autopista Sur surged through bluish diesel smoke. They stood on its shoulder and watched the buses streak by, swerving to wild stops at the raise of an arm. The semitrucks bellowed out their weights, hurrying to the markets and warehouses to drop their loads and get more before the morning rush began. Here was a cement footbridge over the highway Ramón said he should try hard to remember, as well as the crematorium, the empty flower stands, and beyond that, the butcheries.

"Get off when you smell dead cows," Ramón said, waving down his own bus to the north. "Good luck."

Wilfredo counted the change in his hand, raised his arm to a bus with an ABASTOS sign in the front window, and found an empty seat behind the driver. There had been no time to ask the questions he had thought of on the sofa, unable to sleep for more than a few minutes before he woke up suddenly as if already on a bus or tied to a streetlamp or with his back against a hospital wall. From what side of the hill did the sirens sound? Who ran the neighborhood? Gangs? The guerrillas? The paramilitaries? What was the price of fish? He wanted to buy one big enough for everyone to eat.

You throw and you throw, Ramón had told him. It's mud and shit and all these poor pendejos picking up any fruit that falls, and you are not even awake enough to take it all in until later when your wages are spent, dozing off for a siesta and remembering the busy time before sunrise. That's the advantage. You work in your sleep.

Wilfredo followed the men through the arching red gate that said *Corporación Abastos* and out to the lot where the trucks were being guided into slots. He had eaten nothing but a banana, a tight fist in his stomach now. He could not see from one end of the market—towering red bodegas, chain-link fences, wagons, horses, sawdust, and crates everywhere—to the other. The plazas and bodegas were lit by arc lamps. Like on a river, one just had to know the turns, the rhythm, and then he could move right, yet he perceived no order, no line of men with numbers, just the wholesale sellers waving clipboards.

"I'll take three men who can move," one seller yelled, looking for size, something on bones, shoulders, necks.

Wilfredo, unknown to all, was chosen as a thrower. He ran up the loading ramp onto the trailer of a truck, grabbed a burlap sack of carrots and heaved it onto the back of his neck, ran down as a skinny kid with Chinese eyes ran up.

Where to? The seller squinted at him—what? a retard? a moron? The unchosen laughed, eyeing the next truck. The big diesel rigs were rolling in with fifteen-foot trailers and black tarpaulins strapped down over metal arches.

"Do you know where you are?" the seller said.

Wilfredo nodded. The bag was slipping, hunching him over in a way that tested his back.

"New then. It's not hard. Follow el Chino to bodega thirty-one."

"Listo, señor."

Thirty-one? El Chino squatted beneath a bag of mangoes and cussed at the slow-footed black man blocking their path with a dolly of frozen fish. The black man rolled his red eyes, blew a kiss, and let them pass. They seemed to walk in a wide circle to a low canopy and across a court of cratered black concrete, to drop the bags where a large campesino woman was setting up a scale and a table.

"Why so far?" Wilfredo said. "There must be a better way."

"Listen," el Chino said. "If there were a better way, you wouldn't be here. Just learn the numbers today. The numbers, then work tomorrow. Otherwise you ruin your reputation."

"How much do you make?"

They were walking back now, swinging their hands to get some blood into their fingers, almost a run, weaving between carts, other men with boxes, crates, bags on their necks. No one avoided puddles or manure. No one looked up. All was a hurry.

"It depends," el Chino said.

Wilfredo felt a twinge behind his shoulder, which he carefully shrugged off, getting the blood to move. A gray line formed on the horizon. The noise of engines. Cold gasoline wind blew across the many lots. It seemed a miracle even for him to have found the right place to stand, to be working on his second day in the capital.

"Depends if your shoulders stay in their sockets," el Chino said. "It depends on the weather, on how many men there are, how much the seller has left in his pocket after stealing his cut."

The hardest work there is, Ramón had said last night. But there's no shame in working in Abastos. Worse, imagine, would be el botadero.

What's el botadero? Wilfredo had asked.

It's where all these people with wagons and cardboard and scrap metal on their backs go. It's where they weigh the junk and give you some spare change. It's a dump.

"After this, follow me to the next truck if you want," el Chino said.

"I am Wilfredo."

"Grab the lightest bags first. Save your back and walk fast, but not too fast or you unload the whole truck yourself. Watch the other men."

When the truck was empty, Wilfredo shook his arms free of the prickles, the same tickling pain between his shoulder and spine. He accepted the thousand peso bill for twenty minutes of work and bought a little gray plastic cup of coffee for himself and el Chino—two hundred pesos each.

After the second truck the sky was pink, and the arc lights went dark. After the third, the sun rose, and the work was a little more pleasant, but then the pain began. His arms felt numb, too heavy to lift above his waist, and his chest burned from the altitude. It was the speed of the work, not the weight, the sudden arrival of so many trucks that there was no choosing of men in the line. All were needed. They unloaded sacks of corn, yucca, raw green coffee, maracuyá, lulo, potatoes, coconuts, fish, live pigs—food for millions. At one point they were unloading a truckload of potatoes from Boyacá, and he looked at el Chino whose face had turned black with dirt, the shoulder of his flannel shirt torn and wet. They bent their necks under the weight. They moved at a trot because their bodies were giving out.

The trucks came fewer, parked and empty, the drivers looking for loads to elsewhere. The produce and meat and fish stands were packed and splayed with color. El Chino stood with the others in a long line, glaring at the sky. He flagged a truck himself, carrying cages of live chickens for a farmer, hoping for one more load to make the morning count. Wilfredo felt the change in a lump in his jean pocket, a few bills, eight thousand pesos when the bus back to Cazucá was eight hundred. He watched the truck drivers smoke and kick their tires, and saw himself only a week ago retrieving bags of fertilizer from Bagre, paying a no-name thrower like himself to load his panga.

Though fewer, the trucks kept coming. Most were loading, carrying food to the suburbs of Bogotá or other cities. Desperate throwers who had not made their day's wage guided them into slots at the bodegas and jealously guarded the tailgates until the drivers shooed them away or gave instructions. At many of the curbs where trucks had departed was a spillage of oranges, cucumbers, tomatoes, mangoes, papayas, which had fallen or were thrown away by picky sellers. Old men and mothers and children filled up their sacks. Some squeezed off the rotten tops of oranges and bit into the dirty pulp, sucking out the juice.

A teenager displayed an open case of watches. Out in the lot, a fat man in a wheelchair with hand pedals connected to gears, like an upside-down bicycle, wheeled himself fast from one end of the bodega to the next, charging buyers with a credit card swiping machine mounted on his chest.

Wilfredo followed el Chino from one bodega to the next. They were high-ceilinged warehouses with a grid of aisles, little stands and compartments dedicated to one thing. An entire bodega sold cheese and milk and eggs, another corn with live hens in cages. They went through the aisles of meat, long stretches of stomach, rump, and ribs, pigs' feet and tongue sliced onto trays, while the butchers, who all wore white pants and white button-up shirts, were soaked brown with blood, lounging beside the slaughter.

The throwers were done. Most of the time Wilfredo had followed el Chino, and other times he stayed close to men who knew, holding their pace, running into people who cussed him, no longer just sellers on the pathways but buyers from restaurants and grocery stores, hotels, households, soup kitchens, airlines, the whole city growling, bartering, faces scrunched up in amazement at opening quotes and heads snapping backward as if slapped, then shaking side to side, a finger wagging. Up and down the narrow aisles one drama after another played out with affected anger or surprise, and like this the buyers filled their carts.

"Take this, hermano," el Chino said.

Wilfredo drank from a little cup of aguardiente.

"That will get you home," he said.

"I was a panguero," Wilfredo said, "but I lost my business."

"I worked in the emerald mines," el Chino said. "This is better. Let's go see the chickens."

The poultry sellers were women who had colluded in their pricing of chickens, some of which had been injected and inflated to an extreme with water, like grotesque drowning victims, while others had lived decent lives, been fed the right things, and el Chino caressed their heads, pulled on the skin of the breasts, and checked for the two orange eggs inside the hens. "Tomorrow, we'll do better," he said. "Today I have to pay for my son's school."

Between two bodegas was a row of taverns where throwers, sellers, and drivers drank beer, threw dice, and reveled in the stillness, the workday being done. El Chino stepped in and brought back a pint bottle of aguardiente and two little plastic cups.

"Just one," Wilfredo said. "I have to go."

"Maybe tomorrow you will make ten or fifteen thousand, like me. It gets easier when you know. Twenty is possible, it's rare, but it happens, especially on Saturdays. It's better to be careful, save your body for tomorrow."

"I hurt my back already. Look."

He turned and el Chino touched his shoulder with his thumb, then pulled up his shirt to see it.

"Mierda, Panguero, there's an eggplant in your back."

CHAPTER THIRTEEN

MARTA HAD WARNED HER against it, but Caterín squeezed into the new white pants, so tight they shortened her strides. She was glancing between the shacks with that look of the girls who were leaving Cuturú any day for the city and wore their best outfits even to walk to the store or wheel garbage out to the corner. Her hair was wet and her face painted a glittery yellow with the dark eyebrows almost purple in the cloudy light. The three of them had shared the same water for a bath, yet by the time Hernán dipped in, the water was murky, tepid, and he felt coated now in a film of unclean soap.

They crossed the road to Tres Esquinas, a bus hurdling past them, and the driver leaned out the window to hoot at Caterín, "Mamita!" He made the shape of an ass with his forefinger and thumb and licked it. "Qué rico!"

"This way," Caterín said, snapping her piercing against her teeth. Their destination was La Esperanza, the cultural center where Lidia worked. "I have to leave a message with someone."

"It's already eleven," Marta said. "If we don't get there by noon, mamá is going to make a scandal."

"Go then if you want."

"And Hernán?"

"Take him."

"But he needs to meet your beloved," Marta said in an announcer's voice as they entered a downhill alley. "He needs to make himself known. No? We want him to be safe, he's so sweet."

Hernán wore jeans too long for his legs and bunched up at Milton's handed-down shoes. He asked the girls about the black flooded field opening up below them, and Marta laughed excitedly, saying it was the shit lagoon. There had once been crystal water, tended by an angel in a canoe who sang lullabies at night. Now she stacked the dead bodies of the teenagers on the shore. The seagulls had torn loose her nose and her eyes. The gray water of the tanneries and the turds from the sewage pipes had driven her insane, but in the hot vision of drunks, she was still a beauty. She lured them out to drown.

As they hit shore, the sky became huge. The neighborhood, a steep, unused hill only five years ago, could not conceal, even with the bright touches of paint, some potted plants, its impermanence. In the cement or rope bonding of one brick or plank to another, you could see time—the desperation or patience of the builder—as some houses tilted dangerously while others were dug so deep into the hill they looked like mine shafts. Plastic adorned everything—tarps around poles, bags in puddles, airborne or stuck on antennas and foundation rebar.

"What do you think?" Marta said, as they climbed onto a gravel road and approached the cement slab of a soccer court.

"It's humble," he said.

"Look." Marta pointed back again at their blue house. "Up over that hill is Ciudad Bolívar. They have pavement and a library there."

"This is their shit," Caterín said, pointing at the lagoon.

"It's yours, too."

"Shut up!"

"But papá wants us to move to Bosa," Marta said. "He's tired of climbing hills like a goat. He's tired of the paramilitaries asking for his name. Everyone here is so stupid. Some aren't even poor. They just say, Why pay rent in el centro when you can own a piece of land and build on it? Look, there's Cate's novio Antonio."

In the thick of a game, Antonio, a short tough-looking kid, chased a tiny hard ball across the court. He reminded Hernán of a palm tree that had thickened but never grew. He ran with his head too far ahead of him, not so quick, but springing free with loose balls and kicking them down court to a tall black muchacho in clunky work boots. A shortened game, the court just a plaza-sized rectangle.

They walked close to the fence, and the game paused for Caterín. Antonio kissed her, fitting his hands under the waistband of her white pants. His teeth were smashed to pieces with one black upper tooth pointing out like a bug, but he was somehow handsome. Maybe it was his confidence. Caterín stood a head taller than him, surveying the other girls who sat beyond the goal posts, holding hands, pushing each other, hollering for help or to be listened to.

"I'm Antonio," he said, holding out a callused hand for Hernán. "Do you play, primo?"

"A little. Not—"

"Do you want to play now?"

"No."

"Then sit."

Antonio led them over to the spectators beyond the goal post.

"We can't stay," Marta said.

"Cate, you came!" said a thin girl, her face stuccoed with beige makeup. Her hands seemed fractured with cuts, a black scab over a missing thumbnail, but her teeth were white and impressive. "What I ask is who is next? He was on a list. What's crazy is I knew it the second it happened. I told him, I said, You don't stay home when everyone sees it. But why would he listen to me, the only one who loved him? The only—"

"Her novio is dead," Caterín said, introducing her as la Coca. "Where did they get him?"

"Right here." La Coca pointed at a faded black stain in the far corner. "It's an insult to play there."

"She's exaggerating," said a teenager with bleached hair gelled to one side like a shelf, and his was a pretty face of rapidly changing expressions. "He deserved it. He tried to join the paracos. No chance there."

"You heard that?" la Coca said. "Who told you?"

"It's a fact."

The pretty boy reminded Hernán of all the cutureños who left for Medellín and came back with emerald crosses, pistols in their jeans, short tempers, and a disbelief in humans. They talked too fast to be understood. The sounds of their words meant more than the meanings. Here, though, was some clarity on the rules of his new neighborhood. The neighborhoods had borders, the pretty boy said, unmarked but with obvious corners of delineation, key streets instead of riverbanks, and there were gangs in each. Antonio was the leader of theirs, but they all had to bow to the metro paramilitaries who ran most of the hills, cleansing them of thieves, drug addicts, molesters, guerrillas, leftists, or anyone who crossed them. They killed on rumor. On jealousy. On bad blood.

"Who's next?" la Coca said, reaching for the pretty boy. "It could be me or you. Why not?"

"And?" the pretty boy said, his face flickering between bitterness and pleasure. "So it gets hot for a while."

La Coca brought her face close to Hernán's and told him he was lucky to be in Cate's house with the red tiles, the tub she had once pissed in because the toilet had been so dirty and because she was envious. Nothing could happen to you in a house like that. But if he walked around with that curious look, without Antonio's protection, he'd be cut down by the first muchachos to cross him.

"I'm leaving," Marta said.

Caterín's gaze jumped across the lagoon as if to see Lidia descending the hill with a machete.

"If you leave, Cate," la Coca said, "I'm going to die. I'm going to the wake tonight, and then I'm going to get drunk." Tears gelled together in her eyes, and she grabbed at what she said was a heartbeat problem. She had a thousand problems it seemed. "Should I even go?" She had not gone to the morgue, nor had she seen his body on the court. For the wake, she'd wear her black slacks, a black sweater, owning no dress, and would press her lips against the dirty plate glass they put over the coffins. There would be other girls to compete with.

"Give up the joint, whoever's got it," la Coca said, but no one had one.

Marta walked off the court and into the pines. In a few minutes, they saw her crossing the gravel causeway of the lagoon and moving uphill into a neighborhood the pretty boy called el Progreso.

The sky opened up, the sun bearing down on all their necks and faces. The game sped up, but no one watched. The sun made the girls—there were three of them now beside la Coca—uglier. They were not designed for so much light. The boys looked goofy in their hair gelled straight back or straight down. They cracked their knuckles, smoked, sang fragments of songs, saying what was a chimba and what was not. Their eyes skipped over Hernán.

"Why are you here, parce?" the pretty boy said.

"We had problems on the river," Hernán said. "My father was a panguero."

"A wooden boat?"

"No, it was fiberglass."

"What problems? Paracos?"

Hernán nodded but did not elaborate.

"Not a sapo. Good. Cate, your cousin's not a sapo. At least." The ball bounced over Hernán's head, into the pines. "More like a little chicken than a sapo," the pretty boy said, watching Hernán run to pick it up. "El Pollito, let's call him."

"Why does no one care about me now?" la Coca said. "I'm asking for some compassion."

"I gave your cousin a name, Cate," the pretty boy said. "It's el Pollito."

"It's not a bad name," Caterín said, "if he grows."

CHAPTER FOURTEEN

LIDIA WAS DONE WITH HER laughing for the day. She grabbed Caterín by the armpits and, aiming for her chin, belted her across the forehead, a snapping sound, and swung twice more, leaning forward, cocking far behind her head and landing blows to her cheek and neck.

Hernán had never seen a woman punch in combinations. He was trying to eat an inky bowl of purple beets and raw onion.

"Puta!" Lidia said. "Is that what you want to be?"

"Don't hit me," Caterín said. "It's embarrassing."

The white pants were splattered with mud, and an orange spot glared on one knee from a leak in Antonio's roof. Where, Lidia asked, were the pants *then?* They were not on her legs.

Caterín and Hernán had arrived at dusk, blue-cheeked, soaked, and involved, in Lidia's mind, with the grief for some boy who had probably done enough wrong to deserve his death. And to let Marta walk alone up the hill to La Esperanza!

"If I look at you, I will hit you again," Lidia said.

Lidia pulled Hernán upstairs and onto the roof where Alba sat wrapped in a wool blanket, her back against a half-wall of brick waiting for the completion of the third story. She was watching for Wilfredo who was many hours late.

"What a bad second day! Everyone disappearing," Lidia said. "Poor Alba sick and bleeding, and my idiot daughter out fucking a hoodlum. If the women of La Esperanza saw me, what would they say? All day I preach and preach, no violencia, talk to your children, don't hit them."

Walking home from Antonio's house, Caterín and Hernán had joined a traffic of people—maids, security guards, construction workers, and schoolkids—while the policemen on motorcycles made their final loop through the neighborhood and soldiers patrolled with long rifles and battle helmets, a sensational illusion. Propane and beer trucks and buses bounced in and out of the puddles and ruts, splashing houses with mud and struggling up the steep slopes. One truck had clipped the edge of a shanty, knocking down an entire wall, the half-naked inhabitants emerging with kitchen knives.

Now the streets were empty. No buses. You could hear the high-pitched whir of televisions and radios, the doom-da-da bass of ballenato in a cantina. Hernán gazed down at the lagoon, searching for the caretaking angel, but saw only the white specks of seagulls. Where the hills flattened down at la Autopista Sur was a secondary circuit of light flowing around Soacha, once a small town outside of Bogotá, now packed with a million residents.

"Ramón will find him," Lidia said. "Surely he just got off on the wrong corner."

"Surely," Alba said. "He could be anywhere in those lights."

"I know Ramón. Mierda. He never explains things."

Ramón had arrived an hour ago, hanging his suit from an exposed pipe in the living room, cussed at the panguero, and set back out for la Autopista Sur to find him.

"Who was la Coca crying over?" Lidia asked.

"Her novio," Hernán said.

"Who cares? They'll all be dead soon. Watch!"

Caterín appeared in the doorway with a tray of steaming aguapanela. Hernán thought she was too beautiful to look at.

"Here's the girl who wants to be a gamín," Lidia said. "My daughter the streetlamp."

Caterín blinked and ran her hands through her hair.

"Go back downstairs," Lidia said.

Not far from a plot of potatoes and corn by the lagoon, Antonio's house had been built onto a rock-hard ledge, the back side of it brick where the electric cable came down from the power line, the front patched up with sheet metal.

While Caterín and Antonio fucked to the beats of reguetón behind the curtain, la Coca wept some more, her face gouged and smeared by the rain.

He only fucks with music, she said. Well, do you smoke?

Yes, he said.

I only have one. Let's share it.

They sat outside the door and watched rain distort the hillside. Wet and disheveled seagulls hopped around with black beaks. Hernán's hand jittered as he brought the cigarette to his lips without looking at it, pulling just enough to keep it going.

I don't know. Some days I don't know, she said. I wanted to go to the wake but not alone, not if I can't get my good clothes. If I go home, they won't let me leave. Pollito? Do you like that name?

I like it.

The problem is they give it to you and you have to live with it. How old are you?

Thirteen.

That's nothing, she said. Think how much I've suffered in three years since I was twelve. If I told you, you would not want more years. Your luck is to have Lidia and Ramón. They know a lot of people, and Ramón says he's going to open a school. There's money in that.

She told him how she and her family were the fallen. They had moved here from Bogotá. Her father built them a solid house in

Cazucá, then took off with his truck and found another woman in Cartagena. Any day, he'd come back, and she could start night school in San Mateo. His truck was turquoise, a Ford. Maybe he would take them somewhere. Hernán could come. She glanced over her shoulder and whispered that Antonio was nice but evil, how he just wanted to fuck Cate and use people, how she fucked him too when she was bored, which was often. Antonio was head of the gang in el Progreso, she said. If some pandilleros were to show up right now to kill him, then you'd see ten more of ours come out and get them first.

Where is el Progreso? he said.

Here. You live in La Isla. You don't know anything. That's hard.

After a while, Antonio emerged to smoke on the steps. Everyone wanted to teach Hernán. He pointed at different markers among the hills—streets, antennas, a distant tree with no leaves, and asked if Hernán had a knife.

Not over there, Antonio said. Not there either. It looks quiet, but they are crazy. He pointed away from the slum at the town of Soacha. He shook his head. And in Soacha they think they are hard, but do they dare step on our hill? No, parce. We go down there when we feel like it. Do you have a knife?

He doesn't need a knife, la Coca said. She grabbed his thigh and squeezed and leaned into him with her hair in his face.

You care about me, she said. That's all I want.

Careful, Antonio said. Careful with her.

*

Hernán reached out and touched Alba now, surprising her, as if she had not been touched in many days. The three of them sat on separate blocks of cement, a little cold as the sugar high of the aguapanela wore off, and looked down at the street where neighbors trudged uphill, carrying bags of food or uniforms from their jobs in the city. He felt powerful looking down on them. In Cuturú, there were no two-story houses, not even the chapel. You had to climb a tree if you wanted a view.

"Are you mad at Wilfredo?" Lidia said, digging dirt out of the tread of her shoe with a nail.

"No," Alba said. "I don't blame him now. Our father resisted, and he's dead. Either way you lose, and we are alive."

"Poor Hernán," Lidia said. "I wish he could have gone to school in Caucasia. That was a good plan. Up here, one day he won't come home. That's what Cate did to me. I sat right here all night, and I waited. I walked the entire neighborhood, and they told me she had left with that girl Liliana who snorts glue. Four days passed like that, and I thought she was dead. People rape girls up in those hills and bury them. Can you imagine my fear? And then a bus driver in Honda calls to say he found these two stupid girls crying in the terminal. One of them says she is mine. And she is. See?"

"Dios mío," Alba said. "And Wilfredo?"

"Maybe Ramón found him, and they are at the cantina," Lidia said. "Ramón would do that, leave us worrying like bitches."

"Wilfredo is dependable," Alba said.

"With Ramón . . ." Lidia laughed with long gulps of air, pouring her aguapanela over the edge of the roof into the street. "Too sweet for me. You wonder. You ask, Albita, why I am so lonely? Well, this is my routine. I sit on this roof and watch our alley while Ramón is out with other women. He has a business, fine, but if not for that, why stay? I get offers from good men, teachers, store owners. I'm respected. But I think, why move all of my things, just so it will happen again when he gets bored? And what about my girls? The last thing they need is a stepfather."

"Pobre Lidia," Alba said. "It's hard for everyone."

"How many women," Lidia stomped her foot once on the thick cement, "have houses like this? It all sags a little, but Ramón built it. What woman would not give up something? You ride down la carrera Trece in Bogotá, and you see them with their legs open. No?"

"Puro sexo," Hernán said, his first contribution to the discussion, and Lidia laughed harder than her body could handle. She ended up coughing and spitting over the side of the roof.

Pure fucking, Hernán thought, gripping in his pocket the white canoe-shaped clasp-knife Antonio had given him, and he would fuck too. He knew how it worked. In Cuturú, it was Milton's Lucila in the woods behind the soccer field, grabbing the trunk of a tree to keep balance, Milton upon her, saying, te amo, te amo, grabbing the thick burst of hair between her legs, at her nipples over her belly, and she did not mind.

"Tía," he said. "Why don't we build this third floor, and we can live with you?"

"For Ramón to finish this, he would have to do something horrible. If he broke my legs, maybe. I guess I could bear that."

"Is the light over your door different?" Hernán said. "Will papá remember it?"

"There's Tres Esquinas. You aim for those antennas, and you get up here. The worst that can happen is he gets robbed. It's not so bad unless he made a lot of money, and I doubt that. Ramón will find him."

"He's not a fighter," Alba said. "He would not resist."

"I would," Hernán said.

"You?" Lidia said. "You won't make it through school if you do."

She was laughing again. She was never done. She called downstairs and told Caterín no more holding up dinner; they would have to eat something or get depressed.

"Home," Lidia said. "You get used to it because there are a few good people around, and I'm one of them. You'll see."

CHAPTER FIFTEEN

AFTER TWO BUSES AND A DAY of wandering among similar redbrick buildings, Wilfredo wriggled through a barbed-wire fence and approached the burned framework of a house in what seemed a cow pasture. He was near la Autopista Sur and saw the right hill but had no idea where to enter it. He smelled the butcheries, the ash of the crematorium, but where were they? Some teenagers at one of the pedestrian bridges had pointed up at the red antennas of Tres Esquinas.

It's not a good time to go alone unless you take a van, they said.

He asked them to lend him money. He told his story about being robbed by a woman with a gun, but it was not interesting to them.

Un loco más, they said. They looked like woodpeckers with their hair gelled forward. They wore shiny plastic coats and had burns on their hands. They said they were sorry.

Paila, they said. You can risk the walk if you are crazy like us. We walk up there.

Take me then, Wilfredo said.

Not for free. We don't know you, old man.

He lay down in the wet grass. He felt the pulse of the city, all its machinery, its gas and water surging through the ground against the ache in his thighs and shoulders. He heard air brakes and horns, a man shouting numbers at the passing buses. He dozed off. Rain was hitting his face and disappearing in the fabric of his clothes. He sat up and snapped his fingers to scatter some yellow sheep surrounding him. A hallucination? A dark herdswoman poked him with a stick, a pair of jeans knotted around her head, and her eyes lumped with pockets of firelight.

"Buenas noches," he said. "Do you mind if I stay the night in your pasture?"

She was mute, but waved at him to follow her. They crossed over a field of trash and burned undergrowth. Here was a blue tarp strung up between two trees. At its edge flickered a little fire with a pot of water. She pointed at a dry spot of ground beneath the lip of the tarp and he sat.

"Gracias," he said. "I've been lost all day."

"Do you work for the water company?" she said, her voice whiny.

"No."

"I paid, but no water. They call me la Cochina."

"I'm Wilfredo."

"It's not my land. Here I have a tent, and you are welcome to it. Out there, señor, they are people with more contacts than I. Politicos y mafiosos, and they are always armed. Be careful. Where do you come from?"

"Caucasia."

"And now? It's probably better to die of hunger in el campo, but we don't. Are you sure you don't work for the water company?"

CHAPTER SIXTEEN

DAWN WAS THE BEST TIME to be awake in Cuturú. Alba would watch the sun cut low through the green dust of the pines and light up the red buoys on el río Puerco. She would throw feed at the hens and feel the town come alive. Wilfredo would ready his boat at the port, maybe plan a route or check at the grocery store to see who needed a run. He went toward Bagre sometimes with nothing scheduled and could find passengers in the smaller villages on the paramilitary side of the river. He was too generous, worked often on credit, and lent money to Tuts and his other brothers on the coast. If it had been her business, they would have had property and a bank account in Caucasia. She did not possess the brilliance of some women for business, nor a head for numbers, but she had foresight. It offended her that a year ago they had buried and unburied in the back patio a savings of two million pesos and now he begged for work at a market.

She sat now in Lidia's doorway, the house empty. A group of teenagers were holding up the wall the propane truck had knocked down the evening before, while another man stood on a folding chair and pounded nails into flimsy wooden braces at the corners.

Years ago, unhappily in love with another, Alba met Wilfredo at one of the cantinas in Cuturú. Her lover had trouble with the guerrilleros across the river for having sold coca paste to the paramilitaries; he had stood before their council and was expelled. He urged her to depart with him to Medellín, but she knew she was staying, not because he was a graceless lover, for she could live with the strange egoistic sex of men, but more so it was that he had tasted the easy money of the drug traffic. Even if he promised he had construction work in Medellín, she knew the truth. There would be other women. There would be lies, and eventually he would be locked up or shot to pieces she would have to bury. If she went, her father said, he would drag her straight back to Cuturú.

No, she said, I don't dream of the city.

Wilfredo at that time owned a long canoe and a weak four-horse Mercury. He had asked her to dance to Darío Gómez's "Me Atrapaste," and when the song ended they went to the soccer field where all lovers went. In a month, she was pregnant with the first baby she would lose. Her face changed. No chin at all. She lost her beauty the way one loses a full wallet. She had the look of a woman who shovels potatoes for a living, bent forward, strong, built to suffer, but in private.

Her first lover had done so much talking, a man who could find humor in his setbacks, and he bought her jewelry, an orange bikini, a radio, and once took her to a movie in Caucasia. From Medellín, he sent her a few pairs of pink erotic underwear that fit her so tightly they interfered with her digestion. Beyond the silver earrings, Wilfredo had given her no gifts. He was quiet and without opinions—the ideal husband, her mother said, if you don't want to ruin your nerves. Her mother's nerves got ruined anyway after the murder of her husband. She went off to live with Alba's sister in Montería, worse, where there were enough Mancuso paramilitaries on motorcycles to constipate her so much her intestines became knotted and had to be cut every year.

Nerves. How are my nerves now? Alba thought. Although Wilfredo did not beat her, he outweighed her in all decisions, in the lending of his money, in waiting for the final knock in Cuturú, and she endured. She was not like Lidia, not the type of woman who liked to be tied up and punched. She closed her eyes, hearing Lidia's laughter from the night before, spitting off her high roof and bragging about her mosaic tiles, the beef they ate, the times she had gone to the movies in Bogotá. It was childish, Alba thought, but then she was the big sister always.

"Servicio, señora?" asked a thin man in new white tennis shoes, a plastic washing machine roped onto his back. "Two thousand pesos a wash, detergent included. Barato, barato."

"No," she said. "Gracias."

"And when your water runs out?"

"I don't know."

"Well?"

She said nothing, and so he glanced at the impressive house and continued on up the alley, stopping at the next door and screaming: "Lavado a tres mil pesos! Lavado de máquina! Barato, barato! Save time and water!"

If Wilfredo were dead, some spike of heat or cold in Alba's body would tell her. The country doctor had touched her belly, rubbed her neck with eucalyptus leaves, and said the baby would live, but how could he know about the hoods?

Things had always happened on the river. If there was a confrontation, the military patrolling, Wilfredo would spend the night at a pension in Bagre or sleep on any campesino's floor. Or if he ran out of gas or the motor broke—or there were any number of excuses. Sometimes he called Padre Moisés to leave word. If he were any other man, she would feel sure he had lovers, but that was not his fix. He loved working. He hated to be still even for an afternoon and so would accept runs with which he might only break even, riding upriver, wasting gas, just to be moving. He would always come home, but here he might be gone already.

Once the baby had bled its way entirely out of her body, she would adjust, as she might have done thirty years ago in Medellín if she had obeyed her passion—her lover owned a restaurant, she heard, and had seven children, while she only had two.

"Alba."

She felt a hand on her knee. The stench of hungry breath and mud.

Her plan had been to forgive him and be done with it. She did not expect her bitterness. "Wilfredo!" She grabbed his wrists and tried to read his eyes. His clothes hung dark on his body, as if he had been lifted out from a damp hole. He leaned his back against the wall and babbled about sheep and throwers and paramilitaries.

"What a bad start, Wilfredo! What are you saying?"

CHAPTER SEVENTEEN

EVERYONE WANTED TO TOUCH the ruptured disc and feel glad they did not have one. Lidia said it was more like a mango than an eggplant. She tried to stick one of Ramón's sharp needles into it, but Wilfredo convulsed, knocking her backward with his elbow, and he spent the evening apologizing. On the second day, he got up before dawn to return to Abastos, but he could hardly lift the full teakettle to pour water into the coffee filter. Lidia stood in front of the door and sent him upstairs to sleep in the big bed with Alba.

As the girls left early for school and Hernán accompanied Lidia to La Esperanza, busy making cheap jewelry and ornaments for a fund-raising bazaar, the house remained empty. After a morning of staring too hard into the depressing concrete patterns of the second-story ceiling, Wilfredo would lay all afternoon face down on the couch with Alba who caressed his back while they watched soap operas and talk shows.

"Fools," Alba would say to the television screen and spit into the wastebasket. "Who are these ricos?"

The news was bad. El Presidente Pastrana—a rich man with a tan face and slow tongue, always a white shirt in the stiff wind of a helicopter setting him down in the demilitarized zone to talk terms with the guerrillas—was after the Nobel Peace Prize. The guerrillas would not cede and neither would the government, and both were funded by the gringos in different ways. But when the guerrillas hijacked an airplane and kidnapped Senator Turbay, the white plastic chairs at the peace table were tipped over, abandoned. The final straw, el Presidente Pastrana called it. On the news, they kept showing the guerrillas being expelled from the demilitarized zone, and day by day the government uncovered their empire of Jacuzzis and brothels and bullrings and Passport scotch, silk sheets, luxury SUVs.

"Mierda," Alba said. "I always knew."

The new patriots of Colombia did not want peace anymore. Tanks paraded through the capital, and el Presidente Pastrana bragged about his new Black Hawk helicopters and specialized junglas, antiguerrillero platoons, and the advantages of war at all costs. Backstage lurked a new candidate, a short mafioso messiah from Medellín with severe spectacles, a pursed mouth, always speaking crossly and condescendingly at the journalists. Álvaro Uribe Vélez was his name, and he vowed there would be no more photographed hugs for Tirofijo or any comandante of the guerrilleros who, in the new lingo of the gringos, were terrorists.

War on all terrorists was the chant. The people loved it. Peace had not gotten them much.

"At least this Uribe looks more serious," Wilfredo said. "His father was kidnapped and killed."

"He's a paramilitary," Alba said. "I know that face."

In Soacha at the hospital they called el edificio negro, Alba went with Lidia to see a doctor who she also suspected was a paramilitary. He looked at her blood and her battered uterus, said that it was probably a big piece of the placenta the baby had left behind and the doctor in Caucasia had failed to remove it. There was a procedure to scrape and vacuum it out, a little expensive, but necessary.

"It's not natural," Alba said, fearing the doctor would kill her. Her head swayed as she spoke, as if daring contradiction. "And who will pay for it?"

Where was Ramón? That was the question no one asked. He had

not returned since the night Wilfredo got lost, calling just once to say he was sewing a thousand uniforms for a school, and might Hernán learn to help him?

"He could," Alba said.

"Ramón would take him straight to the whorehouse," Lidia said. "No way. That's his dream with a son."

Tuts called with mixed news. He had won an expensive contract from some narcos to furnish a new hotel in Caucasia. He and Milton were working through the night, making beds, vanities, armoires, a stage, an immense liquor cabinet. "He gets tired, and he's slow, too slow, and stubborn," Tuts said of Milton, "but he knows wood and so he will not starve anymore. My only worry is that he punched one of the neighbor girls and broke her jaw. Why would he do that? Well, now he has to pay for it. So how do you like the capital?"

Wilfredo told him it was not as lucky, not as golden as one expected, especially if your skill had been with rivers. The only river was el río de Bogotá, which he had not yet seen but heard it was just a long gutter cutting the city in half, not deep enough for boats. There was also a lagoon he could smell from the doorway, but it was an insult to anyone who had ever cared about water. He spoke briefly to Milton who was melancholy and said, "Pray for me, papá," though Wilfredo did not pray. "Be a good boy instead," he told him.

Thanks to Lidia, the aid workers appeared in their colored vests with logos of various NGOs, yet always the wrong vest. The family never qualified for the right programs—food, housing, medicine, employment—or they did and the funding was tied up, pending, some merger of objectives, some paperwork missing, and so it might be another six months before Hernán could start school. Alba served the vests coffee in the kitchen where they intellectualized poverty and violence, and explained the various methodologies to deal with deep memory from trauma.

Wilfredo was hesitant to tell his own story in simple language, but eventually it was just one vest, hers blue, drinking her coffee with three spoons of sugar. Her name was Olivia. She smoked minty cigarettes, her breasts small as anthills, yet she wore tight shirts to exhibit them. She leaned away from him when he got heated about the betrayal of Cuturú, but she was not afraid. She wanted the worst details, names, times, distances, for her reports and with this he might qualify for some new initiative. He walked her step by step through the torture and killing of the boys.

"I knew the river best," he said with pride when she couldn't understand why he got used, not someone else, by the paramilitaries. "Everyone knew me from Bagre to Caucasia. I never got lost. I never overcharged. I was fair."

Olivia made Hernán do written tests with the television off, flipping through pages of ink blots in which he saw blood, dinosaurs, balls.

"Balls are problematic," Olivia said. "They imply psychosis. I can't explain the dinosaurs. Is he sleeping?"

"He sleeps half the day if he doesn't go to La Esperanza," Wilfredo said. "He likes the kids, I think. He was not a talker in Cuturú, not at all."

"Has he been tested?"

"He would pass those tests."

They did not understand one another. Wilfredo preferred that Hernán was absent when Olivia visited, for Hernán did not like to tell stories of that day or the night of the escape and Wilfredo didn't see why he should have to. Alba said talking to Olivia was a way to lose more blood.

"Fancy. That's how they all are," Lidia said later, laughing so wildly that Wilfredo had to look away. "They love their theories. They love to discover the word you are. They say they can cure you by talking, but I don't really buy it. Olivia tells me I have repressed rage, and I say, What? Repressed? I'll show you my fucking rage!"

A month ago at Caterín's birthday dinner, Lidia had noticed a bottle of Chilean red wine in Olivia's handbag, which seemed destined for the family, but perhaps because Ramón was slurring his stories from too much rum, it was never offered; the label was gold and silver with three medals. "I would have liked to try some wine," Lidia said, repeating this story every few days as if it summed up Olivia and her place in the house.

Beyond their physical problems, Lidia noticed something wrong with Alba and her family. They spilled their food at the table. They said things that made no sense. They seemed to stare at objects longer than normal to place them, as if each were a new vantage point to appreciate their misfortune. They were crippled by slow tongues, struggling to find the word for a coffeepot, a strainer, a hunk of mango on a plate. Bloodless faces. Squinting at obvious jokes. Ennui. Pink ripe eyes rubbed glassy, no matter how much sleep. Sleep led to more exhaustion and lethargy. Avoidance of windows and strict adherence to routine. Alba had a new tic, itching at the same spot behind her left calf and knee, a sudden freezing while she stirred soup or brushed her teeth. She would dig with her fingernails into the fabric of her jeans and pull up the leg and draw blood. "Some bad veins," she said. "Some bad circulation."

Wilfredo fell in love with the tub, the second before immersion, the first touch of hot water to his legs, but it deadened as his body adjusted, the water cooled and his nose picked up the foul smell of the toilet. On the sink sat someone's plastic watch ticking. He could hear it from anywhere in the house, as it urged him to take some action. What? He reached out to touch the cool concrete of the stairway above his head. Despite everything, why not go home? Borrow money from his brothers for a used canoe. Cast from shore. Fix the house. Redig the garden. Paint the chapel. Face el Suizo. Face Puerto Clavel. Don't rot in this tub. But he could not face the neighbors who had betrayed him.

"Wilfredo, what are you doing?" Alba's head poked in like that of a curious cow, and she lifted him out.

One afternoon, Wilfredo mixed bleach with hot water, pouring it over the sink, the toilet, the tub, the floor. He worked at the brown scum of the sink for a half-hour and made little headway against it. He scraped away the encrusted hair on the toilet. It smelled like someone had jammed a dead pig into the piping. He could see years of child and adult feces stuck together at the joining of Ramón's piping with that of the neighborhood, an impossible knot to undo, and he laughed aloud as he scrubbed, imagining it rupturing someday, a geyser of shit spraying across the alley and onto the weak-framed shanties covered in paramilitary graffiti, right onto the gleaming products of the corner grocery. He felt a burst of pain behind his shoulder, like a hinge swinging too hard and tearing.

He lay down inside the wet tub, waiting for it to end, but the spasms were spreading to new parts of his back, and he found himself stuck, calling for Alba who was not home.

Caterín entered in pink pajamas with little hamburgers printed seam to seam, and she believed it was an attack of insanity.

"Tío, are you OK?"

"I was cleaning," Wilfredo explained. "My back just broke. La hijueputa vida."

"Why were you cleaning?"

She reached under his shoulders and tugged him up over the lip of the tub, and he pushed her backward and in his flailing for a handhold gripped her crotch. She scratched at his eyes, screamed, and ran out.

"Perhaps el Señor is testing you," Alba said later, when he was in bed. She knew he had not tried to molest Cate. "He tested Job."

"I'm done with God," he said. "He gives us nothing."

For a couple days Wilfredo learned to crawl. He appreciated the filth of the whole house, looking closely at the divots and defects, at the textures of cement and wood, crumbs, fingernails, threads. He looked into the incurious eyes of a rat beneath the stove. Caterín glared at him distantly. Who could trust the handicapped? He stayed mostly in bed or crawled down to the television where he lay sideways on the couch and stared furiously at the screen.

"Don't try to clean again," Alba said.

"A man should never clean," Lidia said.

Olivia brought new friends in vests, gray and green, in a white jeep with tinted windows; these shouted their locations into their cell phones, shaking Wilfredo's hand too firmly, making him repeat his story. They came to film. They brought white kites for the children on Lidia's block, and Olivia stood with the photographer, asked Wilfredo and his family to put on white shirts for peace and sit on the unfinished third story of the house, looking out at the lagoon. Hernán sat between his parents, freshly bathed, in a denim jacket, Alba with a blanket over her shoulders, holes in her earlobes, still sick but bleeding less.

"Don't smile," Olivia said to them, as the photographer kneeled at their feet. "Look pathetic."

CHAPTER EIGHTEEN

HERNÁN WOULD GO SILENT for hours and then try to say something just to keep people off his back. He did not want to be talked or listened to. Some nights Marta drew a dividing line and butted him off the bed, but others she might wrap herself around his back and lift up the sheet to finger growing hair in his armpits. She showed him the little hairs on her crotch, requesting to see his.

"Love among cousins," Lidia said, "is as old as the Bible. Keep the curtain open."

"Don't do a stupid thing," Wilfredo said to him, and soon they had set up a private bed for him on a pallet in the living room.

When Lidia would put her arm around Hernán in La Esperanza, a two-story cultural center with a little library, toys, three computers, and bright-orange walls, he wanted to grab her soft stomach and tell her how lonely he felt, yet knowing in one look at her laughing face that he better hold back. When she was mad at him or cold, he wanted to run away to Caucasia and beg Tuts to take him on as an apprentice; so much depended on her moods. He pleased her by sweeping out La Esperanza and working diligently at the beaded necklaces and papier-mâché animals for Saturday's bazaar. She treated him like an equal, talking sex and violence with candor, and, La Esperanza being the meeting place for the angry women workshop, Lidia knew all the gossip and all about Caterín's friends: Antonio had impregnated seven girls and, if not for his uncle, a paramilitary, he would have been expelled or killed by one of the girls' fathers; the pretty boy was on a death list kept by his mother's boyfriend, a politician about to open a new school up the hill; some girl got raped by her uncle and fell madly in love with him. Pendejo problems, she called them, and they fascinated her.

Lidia laughed with fire-alarm intensity at the saddest of stories, not because she was insensitive or unhurt by what she heard at La Esperanza, but because this act of being appalled by the unspeakable, the horrific—a son beating down his mother in public, a stepfather raping his retarded stepdaughter, killing her, and then the mother of this child standing by him, in love—was not possible in Cazucá. The more preposterous, the more Lidia laughed, as she did about the ex–army colonel at the top of the hill, a loan shark who ran a gang of muchachos, all of whom had sex with him, and he had floored his house with black marble, put a fountain of the same material at its center. Or when Olivia had organized a neighborhood cleanup day, and in a ditch not far from La Esperanza they had found a number of garbage bags containing body parts, and so they called the police who promptly arrested the man who found the bags, accusing him of being the descuartizador. No more neighborhood cleanup days. The only cleaning was killing. Once mothers of the neighborhood knew that Lidia would listen, that her laughing was a way of feeling, she was sought out, dragged inside for coffee as she walked home from La Esperanza.

Hernán did not laugh yet and had no clear idea how to act. What he knew, what he was most sensitive about, was that his parents were failures. They sat bundled up in their jackets all day on the couch. Alba did not cook. Wilfredo was just now walking again. While Marta and Caterín finished books and wrote essays, he woke up each morning knowing nothing more than he had known the day before.

"A la cárcel," he found himself yelling on the day of the fundraising bazaar, shoving human plastic figures into the different openings of a foam-block structure. He was older than his playmates, some drooling, one twitchy with a copper earring, ages all confused in that room—even the babies had old-man looks as they added stories and extensive wings and courtyards to the construction of this prison.

Outside, Lidia managed the women and children who sold jewelry, overalls, thick sweaters, baby pajamas, velvet hats with fake feathers. The rancheras of a nearby cantina whined against and overtook the chipper flutes of the children's music playing inside.

Wilfredo sat down on the green slide of the mini indoor playground, observing the children with an overserious, baffled look. He was rammed into by a little girl who streaked down the slide on her belly, scared when she saw him wince. She ran across the room, colliding with the foam construction of the prison, all the dolls flying out.

"All you see is a river, Panguero," Ramón said. A serpent's head of wet hair bobbed on his forehead, and he wore a white creased shirt with a gold tie.

They went upstairs to sit in chairs torn from school desks, colored by children, in the doorway of Lidia's office. Between them stood a single bottle of Ron de Santa Fé and two white mugs. The night before, Ramón had knocked on the door of the house he had built. He brought ten pink tulips for Lidia, a white blouse for Caterín, and a Mexican Barbie for Marta.

Lidia had just stared at the television while he kissed her ears, and when he got down on his knees, she poked his chest, and he rolled backward, scattering change over the cement. He smiled up at the brown veins of cement on the ceiling and blew kisses at all the walls.

"It's a privilege to drink with a friend," Ramón said now, lifting the bottle. "How much is your life worth? It's hard to know when things are this bad."

Wilfredo shrugged.

"I know it," Ramón said. "All we are is numbers in the capital. I know. I've been where you are sitting, Panguero. So what are you going to do? It's time for something. Lidia tells me you sleep all day."

"I should be at Abastos right now, if not for my back. Maybe in a week—"

"Forget Abastos. If you are waiting for things to cool down, then it's time to return to Cuturú. If not, I have a contact in el centro who can get you merchandise. You sell what's cheap, whatever he has. I'll lend you the money to start. You start Monday, you learn."

"I can't sell."

"You know how I began? I walked door to door in Bogotá selling laundry detergent. They spit in my face, and I'm still an optimist. Listen. Let's get drunk."

"Monday."

"Monday. Use Hernán."

"And what with Olivia and the schools?"

"Olivia!" Ramón wiped sweat from his eyes and lowered his voice and whispered, "Wake up, Panguero! She's with the guerrilleras."

CHAPTER NINETEEN

WHAT HERNÁN EXPECTED of a city—storefronts, sidewalks, garbage cans, empanadas frying, bad traffic—was here on the corner of la Autopista Sur. He shaped his wet hair with his fingers while Wilfredo bartered with an arrogant bus driver to let them on at half-price. The seats were old, the springs poked out, squeaky. The bus went slower than the pedestrians, as the driver looked to load up.

Wilfredo had written down the phone numbers of the house and La Esperanza on the back his hand where Ramón had bitten him the night before.

Lidia is just a puta, Ramón had exclaimed and tore apart the blouse he had made for Caterín, so drunk after the bazaar and all day Sunday, everyone staying out of his way, plugging their ears when he yelled about how it was a privilege to know him. Wilfredo sat in front of the television that was all static, making sure Ramón stayed put. Atop the television leaned a single pink tulip in a jar, which Caterín grabbed and threw against the wall. Little pieces of glass scattered as far as the kitchen. Hernán pulled a speck from his hair. Ramón writhed off the couch and tried to kick her.

Touch me, papá, Caterín yelled, and Antonio will kill you.

Her lipstick had smeared up her cheek like one red whisker.

Every time you have a good bazaar it ends like this, Lidia said, peeling a potato nearby and laughing.

When Ramón said it was a privilege to be his wife, Lidia put down the knife, lunged forward, and hit him with her fist, using her legs and hips for power. He fell forward into the stack of red tiles, tore down a new poster of the beach, and then spun around scratching the air. Wilfredo twisted Ramón's white collar tight around his neck like he would the painter of the panga around a tree, and elbowed him down into the cushions, and that was the end of it.

"Look," Wilfredo said. He pointed at a herd of yellow sheep in the pasture. "I slept out there."

They passed the crematorium, bright with flower stands, mourners in black pants and shirts. A thin flume of smoke uncoiled from the brick chimney. The butcheries were busy, the sweet copper smell of blood, the sunlight like white pins on every surface. Men with thick green hoses sprayed down the cement and the hung carcasses. The traffic jammed, and there was selling anywhere people stood still. They passed a military school, English institutes, a bottling factory, and the Mustang Tobacco factory, which smelled like burning chicken broth. Hernán asked Wilfredo if he had seen all this on his lost walk, and he said they could be anywhere. It took an hour to get into the higher buildings, and when they were closer it seemed like the driver was having a nervous attack. He braked hard in the middle of intersections for more passengers and swerved around other buses doing the same. If you pass the highest white bank tower, el Edificio Colpatria, Ramón said, then you went too far.

How high? Hernán had asked.

It had been morning then. Ramón, sober, his biggest gold cross on his neck, was making breakfast for Lidia and the girls. He hugged Hernán and apologized. He shook Wilfredo's hand. Today they forgot. Today they swept up and repaired the torn blouse, and Ramón promised Lidia a new blender. I've been such a gonorrhea, he said. Everything about me is satanic.

They went too far. Hernán stepped onto the curb and looked down at his new shoes, bright white with black stripes, imitation

Adidas, which Lidia had given to him the day before at the bazaar. They walked south on la carrera Séptima toward the heart of el centro, into the shadow of the skyscrapers, some of old limestone and redbrick, some of fancy blue glass. No one looked up or at any one thing. The air smelled like ice cream melting, hamburgers, propane gas leaking from some portable vat of herbal tea. The crowd quickened, fought for space as la carrera Séptima narrowed to a one-way street.

"Llamadas! Llamadas!" called girls with cell phones chained to their wrists, the price of a call printed across their breasts. "Calls! Calls!"

"Stop! Stop! Displaced from el Cauca!" A dirty, barefoot woman held up her pink-skinned baby in just its diaper. "Help for the displaced! Help me someone! God will pay you back!"

No one stopped. The beggars stank like old piss and ketchup, curled up in doorways, thrown against lampposts. Some were women with breast-feeding babies on exhibit, some men with raw red stumps for arms and legs, one with a pus-caked bullet hole in his waist, while one with his eyes gouged out played a jolly tune on the accordion.

Perfumed young men in tight jeans passed out cards for the whorehouses—two for one—pictures of cowgirls with horsewhips, schoolgirls in flannel skirts, black girls in pink underwear, tight-suited office girls.

Hernán and Wilfredo took the cards politely. They waited to cross on the busy corner of la avenida 19; their eyes itched, and they picked soot from the rims of their nostrils. Wilfredo gazed at the traffic as if studying the current of a river. The plan was to work long days for months until they had saved money to rent a space in Cazucá. They would open a store and live behind it. When the store started paying, Wilfredo would put money down on a truck. When he had a truck, he would move freight like he used to on the river, but safer and able to go from one end of the country to the other in a matter of days.

Some walkers sprinted out among the traffic, risking their lives to keep moving. When the light turned green, the intersection remained impassable. They crossed in a surge, zigzagged through the hot engines, a pedestrian wave of baking cologne on suits, perfume in hair, snappy black pants, tight skirts, the ticktack of high heels. A man shouted his location into a cell phone.

La plaza de Bolívar opened up to the blue sky, a broad stretch of yellow flagstones, the justice building, the palace, and an old cathedral with soot on every curve. They drew crosses on their chests.

"Hola," Wilfredo said to a man pushing up a cart of chips, cigarettes, and candy, a cell phone chained to his wrist. The man had a red beard and four fingers on one hand. He was tricky with his missing finger, Ramón had said, so they should convince him to front them the merchandise. No deposits with him. Be firm. "Soy Wilfredo."

"Mucho gusto," the man said in a high, grouchy voice. "Bad luck, bad luck. Here all the way from Cuturú. I know that town. Do you want ties or alarm clocks?"

"Excuse me?"

"Tomorrow I can get something that moves. For now, I recommend the alarm clocks. They draw attention. Ties are slow. Besides, if you have to run from the police, they get dirty and you owe me."

"The police?"

"Listen, Panguero. You can't work asleep. Eyes open! Eh? The mayor wants to beautify the city so the police come and arrest all the sellers. Eyes open! All the way from Cuturú! What a shame! Welcome to Bogotá."

*

"Despertadores!" Hernán yelled before the colored pyramid of clocks on la avenida Jiménez, a colonial street with old brick flagstones and fountains of green stagnant water. "Look! Damas y caballeros! Look, look, look, ladies and gentlemen. For the kitchen! For the office! For the bedroom! So many uses! Don't be late! Wake up!"

Hernán knew how to sell.

"My back is killing me," Wilfredo bitched, pacing around the display. "Can you stand alone if I take a walk?"

"Go, papá. I'm fine."

An old man in pure black crouched down at the pyramid. His eyes floated behind thick glasses, and there was a residue of dried spit on his lips. He stared with longing at the ticking needles.

"Don't be late," Hernán said.

"Hombre!" he reached out a flabby hand. "Here we are. What a noise! They wake up the devil."

"You want a clock, señor?"

"I'm desperate. I'll take three clocks, muchacho! I might be old, but I'm ready."

*

The next morning they reclaimed their spot with an open suitcase full of cigarettes, candy, and chips. They sipped coffee from little gray plastic cups bought cheap from a man who carried a giant steel urn on his back. Hernán did more business when Wilfredo took walks; people had sympathy for working children.

The customers talked openly to Hernán, they gave advice, and asked him about school. They too drank coffee, too much, their eyes red, they said, from staring at computers and numbers that would never add up. They called Wilfredo el Panguero, asked politely about his river, the war in the region. Who to blame? they said. It's the corruption. Maybe if Uribe won the election. At least a change of strategy to kill some people.

At dusk, when a day of selling added up to little, Wilfredo imagined an alarm clock ringing for the day workers to go home and the nocturnal, the thieves and whores, to wake up and descend from the hills. He saw Milton in the bodies of the tattooed punks who sat at one of the fountains all afternoon. He called Tuts to ask about work, and Tuts said he knew a man who ran a dredger in Quibdó. Don't come home, he said. He'd bumped into el Suizo in Caucasia. Milton was laying low, spending all his money on girls.

The hardest moment was early in the morning when Ramón scraped a razor down his cheeks, the teakettle whistling, and Wilfredo awoke in a strange house that did not belong to him. He reached over and squeezed the loose skin of Alba's stomach. She would rub his neck with her thumbs, knowing all the right spots, still time before Ramón washed the foam off his face, stepped over them to turn on the television.

"Seven guerrilleros were killed in a confrontation on the road from Cali to Buenaventura," the morning television said. "Las FARC deny any casualties. . . . One question the presidential candidates have been unable to answer is what to do about the millions of displaced in our cities . . . while General Montoya declares he will return them to their lands, by force, the others are less willing to commit themselves to any program."

After dusk, el centro became a haunted place for the day people. No more lingering in store windows or smoking cigarettes at the fountains. The suits hurried to their taxis and buses with fear. Hernán became a menace in their eyes, walking behind a suit or a smartly dressed woman, their heads snapping backward to eye him. Often they crossed the street. There was less traffic then, the buses heavy with sellers and maids and guards who descended at the bare corners of la Autopista Sur for the long walk up the hill into Cazucá. Wilfredo and Hernán passed the frying empanadas, tempted but hardened to them, feeling the scrape of earned money in their socks. The uphill paths into Cazucá were deserted, lit by broken seams of streetlights and pocketed with darkness. If they saw a group, they detoured, losing and regaining their route, always guided by the black spill of the lagoon. Lone walkers would dodge them too. The recyclers with nothing to lose rode downhill in rough carts behind exhausted horses on their way to the wealthier corners of the city.

"The slave is here," Marta would say.

Hernán would not even look at her. She knew nothing of silence in night buses after the national anthem had played, or the life of those streets, her bare feet soft in blue sandals, her homework done. Every day pushed him further below her in school. He felt like one of those zucchinis that had not been picked in time and matured to a grotesque and unappealing size.

"She's jealous," Caterín would say, staring at the television or a mole on her arm. "We are all so bored with school."

"It's that last climb that breaks us," Hernán said. "The selling is not bad."

"Come earlier tomorrow," Caterín said in warm moment. "It's not about you. It's us who have to wait. The neighborhood is hot. There's a new list of muchachos to kill."

"Los paracos would never mess with Hernáncito," Marta said, reaching out to feel the muscle on Hernán's arm as he sponged off the false leather of his false Adidas shoes. "Look at him now. He's growing. He's not a thief or a druggy. He's fine."

"He's young," Caterín said.

The neighborhood was hot because it was like this every year when the paramilitaries did their December cleaning, leaving the dead in doorways as gifts to their mothers and wives. Sometimes they cut them up. Most times, though, they chased them down the streets and sprayed bullets into groups on the corners, two-for-ones, they called them, announcing in this way that the neighborhood was theirs.

Two months passed in similar ways. Sun in the morning, showers in the afternoon, and always a cold night. El centro lost its newness.

Hernán's birthday was in a week; he would be fourteen, an age at which he might have crossed the river to Puerto Clavel to join the guerrillas or be sent to live with Tuts for his schooling. Under heavy rain when they had to take refuge under the awning of el Hotel Continental, he found himself thinking of Milton and was shocked at how completely his brother had disappeared. They had never been close, for Milton feared that any relation with the younger would make him less macho. Hernán could not love him. He apologized to God. He resented that Milton lived a man's life in the sawdust and machinery of Tuts's shack, that he might have access to one of the pretty girls in Caucasia, that he might have real money in his pocket.

Some nights the house was asleep when they arrived, the road darker, and even the dogs were subdued, aware of some spell on the hill. They avoided the streetlamps altogether, and Wilfredo once pulled his knife on a dark tree they had never seen before. They each stepped backward, as if the tree had eyes. Alba would open the door and did not complain. She lit the stove, lying back down on the pallet by the television, and by the time they had their shoes unlaced, the food was about ready.

"Make it hotter, papá," Hernán would say.

"How hot?"

"Burning."

"Fine."

They watched the soap operas with the girls in silence, and in every overdone scene of love and jealousy in Bogotá apartments, they saw the sky above la avenida Jiménez. Alba's smile dangled on her face. She tried to say encouraging things but did not finish her sentences. Wilfredo told her to buy soap, and, por favor, socks, because their feet smelled nasty and their toes had bled and blistered from walking. They awoke to the alarm clock and moved back down the hill even before they had had a chance to be home.

La avenida Jiménez did not change its course. It curved each morning and evening from the green mountains down through the glass and limestone buildings, and after fifteen long blocks it dumped into the filthy brown smog of la avenida Caracas.

Hernán followed the routines of the suits, the dealers, making this a game to kill the time. He saw the urban guerrillas addressing each other in fake names, exchanging a paperback novel of data and instructions. One morning, before anyone was fully awake, a muchacho rolled up on a motorcycle, drew a pistol, and the side of a teenager's head sprung loose into a fountain. The police taped off part of the avenue, the news cameras came, and no witness emerged.

Hernán took his own walks. He snuck beneath the awning of la Librería Lerner and into the aisles, followed by the eyes of a clerk. He touched the glossy spines and took down the heavy book with Alejandro Obregón's paintings of barracudas and condors and conquistadores and oceans. He licked his lips, asked how much to the clerk—if they are reading, they are not to be asked to leave, the owner had ordered—who said politely and seriously, "Three hundred thousand pesos, muchacho." Lidia's salary for a month, liters of gasoline for their old motor, months and months of selling on la avenida Jiménez, and so he hoisted it carefully back into its slot.

"Adiós," Hernán said to the clerk, looking back at his indent on the black leather chair.

Alonso, a talkative gay barber, smoked menthols with style and said one day he would like to own a club in which everyone smoked with style, him at the doorway deciding who had it, who not. Likely no one would be let in, so he would never own that club. A fang of gelled hair hung between his eyes, and he laid out a plastic plate of chicken guts for the seagulls.

The policemen, bored to tears, their faces spoiled by pimples, asked Hernán what he thought about the seagulls and gay barber.

They smoked, swinging white sticks, seeing the evening thieves at work but too sick of life to arrest them.

Hernán observed the humans of the avenue moving according to unsaid rules that kept each at a distance even when they were bumping shoulders on the corner, beside the tragic frowns of the unemployed, the hated, the indigent, the indigenous, the outcasts, the ones who needed a spot of glue to snort, the ones who sucked cock in the alley or rented their newborns to beggars on their way to richer corners in the north, and those who used makeup or acrylic paint to give themselves stab and bullet wounds, or those who had real ones, real pus, real gangrene, the smell making the difference. You needed a hook, anything. He was proud to know such rules himself.

One day, when Hernán was yelling about a wheelbarrow of avocados, Wilfredo stopped him. He gave him a piece of chocolate from their case and told him to sit down at the fountains.

"I don't know when," Wilfredo said, "but soon, maybe when you are in school, I'm going to leave. It's best for everyone. You might have been a panguero on a better river, but I wanted you to be more. I still do."

"When?" Hernán said. "How will I know?"

"I'll call. Maybe in a year or two, I'll have enough for a truck. I don't see why we would live here. I hate Cazucá. Tuts says he can help me a little. When you have vacations, you can ride with me. Look, I got her the earrings."

So similar to the others, simple drops of silver, but Hernán told him they were beautiful. There was no question of telling Alba. She could not handle even the most neutral information. He had one wish, which was to know the moment when Wilfredo left, to be ready for it. He didn't want him to just vanish.

The sunset that day was endless, the air on the avenue gradually turning to a bluish purple. You could see the thieves coming north from the hills, but Wilfredo and Hernán worked into the dark, walking north from la avenida Jiménez to a better neighborhood, until the last of the avocados were sold.

"There's other news," Wilfredo said, making change for a rich man with lizard shoes. "Milton left Tuts. I don't know where he is. It seems like he joined the military. Don't say anything to Alba."

CHAPTER TWENTY

RAMÓN LOVED TO THROW a party, in part to show off the house, but almost always his mood went sour a couple hours into things. He would imagine himself slighted or he would see Lidia dancing too happily with a neighbor, and he would throw everyone out. His friends did not mind. Ramón bought the booze, cleaning out the till from his tailor shop in Bogotá and convincing Hernán that his fourteenth birthday, his first in the capital, was significant.

It fell on a Saturday. Ramón bought a fifty-bottle case of Águila beer at Tres Esquinas, and Lidia roasted a rump of beef in a big pan in the oven. She borrowed extra speakers for the stereo, put a pink shade over the single bulb in the living room, and the girls admired their pink-tinted bodies as they cleaned and cleaned until the house smelled more like bleach and lime than shitty plumbing, as if, Marta said, it were a skyscraper apartment in Bogotá.

"It's all worth it for a night," Lidia said.

The river men, both friends and strangers from el río Puerco, arrived early, always a little surprised at the size of the house whose walls you could push on without moving them. They wore white collared shirts and blue jeans, their voices rising up in pitch as they drank, closing their eyes to sing along to the old music. One man slapped a cowbell with a stick, another shook maracas. The wives with windburned faces, their hands chewed up from the cleaning work they did in the city, tugged the men onto the dance floor.

Alba danced a bolero with Ramón, her new earrings centering her ears with light and rendering her a more complete woman, wearing not the old yellow dress with red palms—she had cut it to rags—but a new pair of black jeans and a simple white blouse with an open neck. She had found a temporary job at a fruit salad counter in Bogotá where she was not allowed to sit. At home, after twelve-hour shifts, she lay on the cold living room floor with her stocking feet raised high against the wall, rubbing the calf veins and watching the blood come down. She outearned Wilfredo. Into the lining of the red suitcase brought from Cuturú, she hid some savings in hopes of renting a little house up the street, for she had no illusions about opening a store.

When the song ended, she slammed back a little plastic cup of rum. She took Wilfredo's hand for a dance.

"A toast," Ramón yelled, interrupting the music, and slipped Hernán a little shot glass of aguardiente. "A toast to Hernán! To better days, hermanos! Salud! Salud!"

"Salud!" said Hernán.

"Salud!" said Lidia.

"Salud! Salud!" the river men followed.

There came a loud knock. Ramón turned down the music and shouted through the door that the knocker identify himself. They heard the voice of Antonio.

Ramón opened, greeting Antonio with a little surprise at his black tooth and stature, always imagining Cate would choose a taller, luckier muchacho, but for tonight he completely accepted him and the pretty boy and la Coca to whom he handed beers.

La Coca snuck quickly into the bathroom to return wet-faced and hair-styled, smelling of Caterín's deodorant. She took Hernán's hand for a dance. She had no gift for him because she had been kicked out of her house, but she promised something soon. The grown-ups clapped as he twirled her and leaned into her, but the other muchachos were not big on this music. They liked dancing, but preferred the hammering repetitions of reguetón. Once introduced to the guests, they slipped upstairs to the bedroom, pleased to look down from the makeshift terrace on the night streets.

Caterín's white pants had slightly yellowed from use. She wore a perfume sample she had torn from a magazine. Before the knocking, she had been flirting with one of the river men, and now Antonio seemed to her very much a piece of the street. His hair was oily, he had not brushed his teeth, and he brought with him only his repetitious small talk, bragging of a recent fight with a gang at the foot of the hill. Suddenly his toughness was not sexy, and the rumors—his seed ruining over six girls uphill in Luis Carlos Galán—were obviously true.

Her detachment worsened as he laid her across her parents' bed. She let him grope under her shirt, suck on the moles of her neck, nothing new, as he stretched out the waist of her jeans to reach in there. She was dry. Her pulse was low, and he felt it. He knew he was grasping an empty body. So he drove his tongue deeper into her throat, twisting his knuckles against her crotch, the same tricks that had never worked in the first place.

They stopped to smoke outside with the others. She watched him as he sidled up to Hernán and handed him a second knife as an unplanned birthday gift, then showed him how to use it, the soft spots to aim for, the ways to fend off an attack, how to handle a tall, fat, or strong guy, how to find a weak point in anyone. He moved to Marta, running his hand through her hair, sniffing it, letting his hand fall down along her spine. That fast, Caterín saw it, as if she were looking over her shoulder, on her way to Bogotá.

Downstairs sounded a cheer for another round of rum—or for anything, just being together in that moment with the music, which erupted upward through the stairway and the floor in the sound of the shaking cowbell.

"I'm happy for you," Caterín said to Hernán, whose scholarship had come through. His uniform hung next to her own in the closet downstairs. Olivia came through.

"We all need to study," Antonio said. "I'm self-educated, but that's not enough."

A scream sounded below. No, it was happy. It was Ramón, changing the song to a favorite cumbia.

"I'm tired," Caterín said.

"Then we'll go. It's late, mi amor. Vamos, parce!"

La Coca was being dry humped by the pretty boy, propped against the pillows of the bed, and looking at the poster of Jesús Cristo, as if he were on top of her and not your everyday ordinary muchacho. She looked dazed, high on something stronger than pot, not really interested in her lip being bitten.

The pretty boy pushed her to one side, straightened his jeans, and said, "Entonces qué, parce?"

"Vamos. These girls want to sleep," Antonio said.

"Sleep? It's a party."

"I'm staying here," la Coca said, buttoning her shirt and checking her face in the mirror. "Can I?"

"You can share my bed," Caterín said.

"Disgusting," the pretty boy said.

The pretty boy would follow, he actually liked walking the streets at night, but he looked forlorn as they went downstairs, glancing at the television without sound, the pink light, the grown-ups all drunk and crammed onto the couch or leaning against the wall, and knew that something key had always been withheld from his life, that it was all here. He would probably never get it.

Antonio kissed the side of Marta's mouth, said it was an accident, and made a joke of it. He and Caterín stared at each other. She took them to the door, told them to be careful, and locked it with all three bolts. But why these tears in her eyes?

A neighbor had passed out in Hernán's bed so he slept with Marta like old times. It was warmer being off the floor, close to her. The neighborhood seemed then a silent, livable place. No one burned garbage or screamed; the breeze off the lagoon smelled a little like water. Marta leaned her nose into Hernán's cheek and clutched his hand to her hip. They were the forgotten, the ineligible of the sexual games of the night. He heard feet slapping across the tiles, then Alba grunting as she vomited explosively in the bathroom. He stood up to bring her water, but paused before the door when he saw her lunging forward with the heaves, the vivid spread of her ass in the gray dark.

"Kiss me," Marta whispered, when he returned.

"No," he said, touching his lips to her ear.

"Go to sleep," Caterín said, la Coca unconscious beside her. "Your birthday's over."

CHAPTER TWENTY-ONE

WILFREDO WOKE UP much earlier than usual, saying he had to pick up a wagon of mangoes at Abastos to sell in el centro. It was a lie. He went there to throw crates, and his plan was to never sell anything again, to lie to Alba each morning and throw and throw despite his back. Today was a lucky day, as the trucks kept arriving, and for a time he worked side by side with el Chino. Only twice, he went to the wrong bodega, leaving a sack of corn, gladly accepted and stolen, with another seller, which then created a number of problems, until he got it back.

When they had finished, Wilfredo heard a woman yelling, "Quién carga? Who carries?"

He ran for her, picking up two huge sacks of potatoes, one across his neck, the other hugged to his chest, and followed her out the front gates to a station wagon. He slammed the sacks down hard.

"Cuidado, señor!" she said, handing him two thousand pesos. It was too much and he stared at her waiting for the next stop, but she just got into the driver's seat, looked back, and said, "Gracias! Que te vaya bien."

"Muchas gracias!"

How childish to be so excited by so little money, but he celebrated by buying a pint of aguardiente to share with el Chino. They went to see the fish, spread out gray, white, pink, eyes open, on ice. The fishmongers were the most aggressive he had ever seen, spouting prices in singsong voices. He touched the mouth of a red snapper, checked the yellow eye, and figured it had to be a couple days old, the same with el boca chico, the trout, the catfish, all a little frozen.

"A la órden! I'll cut one open for you," a fishmonger shouted. "Which one? No obligation to buy, señor."

"No," Wilfredo said. "I'm just looking."

The prices were too high. They went to a table with carp, brown and grimy. This is my budget, Wilfredo thought, wishing to bring something good back to Ramón's house—but a fish that eats mud and tastes like cardboard? He wandered back to the saltwater fish and pointed at a red snapper. "How much?"

"With a special discount for you, señor, ten thousand pesos."

The fishmonger tossed it onto the scale and snapped his fingers to loosen a plastic bag from a rack above his head, assuming the sale was made.

"I have only eight," Wilfredo said.

"Take a smaller fish."

The man shook his head and looked for a new customer to draw in. He was unshaven, a red bandana across his forehead, cheeks pale as the boca chico, licking his catfish mustache and ruby-red lips.

"Nothing worse than being swindled," the fishmonger said. "Eight thousand, señor. Straight from the blue waters of the coast. But come back next time!"

Wilfredo handed him five worn bills with change, and the man tossed the fish into a white plastic bag. "A la órden, señor."

"You eat like a rich man," el Chino said.

"A gift. We live with my wife's sister. It's not easy."

*

The throwers, el Chino included, were drunk. At noon, the sun flashed out, turning Abastos into a desirable gallery of color, but as soon as Wilfredo unbuttoned his flannel, tasted sweat on his lips, this breath of heat was gone. Darkening the market, the orange brick buildings around it, the sky turned violent with messy clouds. Covered in potato dirt, he had to get home early and sober to bathe before Alba arrived. He was late. He told el Chino he would see him at dawn tomorrow and believed he would.

"Discúlpeme, señor," Wilfredo said to a bus driver with an unfamiliar sign in the window. "Do you pass by Cazucá?"

"Close," the driver said.

"You go by la Autopista Sur?"

"Yes, of course."

There were familiar sights on the side of this road. The Mustang Tobacco factory and a large clothing store. They approached a series of green signs, a clover junction of highways paralyzed by traffic, and now, under a spell of the bus's engine, the zippy voice of a radio commentator, a teenage girl laughing into her cell phone, he dozed off.

When he awoke, a pretty woman with bruises around her eyes, a sack of rotten tomatoes in her lap, sat beside him. Rain blurred all the windows; the aisle lights glowed yellow on the ceiling. Outside was a uniform landscape of orange brick—a bulldozer peeled back a sidewalk, and a herd of cows grazed in a small green lot.

"Excuse me," he said to the woman. "Could you tell me where we are?"

"We are in Usme," she said.

"Near Cazucá?"

"That's behind us."

He looked between his legs, under the seat, and stood up.

"Excuse me, excuse me"—and he stepped into the aisle. He dropped onto his hands and knees, looking through the pillars of feet, then crawling along the wet rubber floor.

"My fish," he said. "It must have slid to the back."

He searched the staring eyes, the passengers not alarmed or interested in a man either crazy or robbed for being inattentive, noting the raw out-of-town look on his face, as clean and simple as the corn and soybean grids of the countryside. To pity him one would have to pity them all, and they had no energy left for it. They had losses of their own.

He walked the aisle, leaning over to check laps and between seats. A teenager elbowed him—"Step back, old man"—and looked away. Most eyes were following him still. Their faces were secretive. They had robbed him together and divided the fish into pieces.

Little by little the passengers descended. He stared at their legs, their pockets, the bulges in their sweaters for the shape of his fish. Past Soacha, and past a long green lagoon, the buildings flattening into shacks, barbed-wire pasture, and junkyards, they stopped at a junction where the semis and long-distance buses zoomed past. The driver eyed Wilfredo through his mirror and pulled into a muddy lot where heavy rain splashed down into the puddles.

"Señor," the driver yelled through the divider. "We arrived at Sibaté, the end. You missed your stop."

Wilfredo walked to the front and looked through the thick plastic glass. The driver wore a black rock-and-roll T-shirt and black leather pants, and had decorated his dash with little depictions of both the Virgin and half-naked women hunchbacked from the size of their breasts.

"I believe in God," the driver said, facing Wilfredo in his mirror. "I'll take you back for free, but you can't just ride all day. Eh? Adónde va?"

"No. Gracias, señor."

Wilfredo jumped onto the pavement. The cold rain poured right down his neck, and his head ached from the alcohol and nap. He rubbed water into his eyes to wake up. Across the street was another lot packed with the chassis of old buses and taxis, where cows, indifferent to the weather, were biting for the slightest tuft of grass. An air pump droned. *Llantería,* said the sign tied to the scrap-metal awning. A boy leaned forward on a stool and took note of Wilfredo on the sidewalk.

"Buenas tardes, señor," the boy mumbled, his face streaked with dirty oil.

"Buenas tardes," Wilfredo said. "Excuse me, but if you could indicate the route away from the city."

"Cómo? Away from the city or to the city?"

"To leave. Is it that way?"

"Papá!" The boy glanced behind him as a little white-haired man with a stiff leg hobbled out, a black wrench in his hand, his face black too from patching tires and crawling beneath trucks, and the boy whispered, "Un loco. He wants to leave the city."

"Buenas tardes," el Llantero said. "The city's behind you." He squinted at Wilfredo, leaning all his weight on his good leg.

"Bien, señor," Wilfredo said, "but what is the route?"

"You are south of Bogotá. You can take a bus on this same highway. It will take you to Fusagasugá, then Melgar, Girardot. Where do you want to go?"

"That's hot land, no?"

"Hot. Too hot."

"I don't know any of it. I'm not from here."

El Llantero stepped out into the rain and pointed over his shack into the gray sky and then at the road that already curved in descent past a conglomeration of white-tarp greenhouses and into the tropics.

"I see it. Muchas gracias," Wilfredo said.

"No, no, de nada. Suerte, señor, but you'll get run over on that road. Take a bus."

"Gracias."

Wilfredo hurried past a roadside café, aware of roasting chicken and frying potatoes, aware of el Llantero's eyes, as black and dirty as the tires he fixed. The llanteros were low but in their station here and with dignity. He was not. He walked in the opposite direction of his family and the shame of the city. He was firm in his decision. The next bus would take him off the mountain.

CHAPTER TWENTY-TWO

WILFREDO DID NOT come home from work in el centro. The first
day they had waited by the television, its screen cracked from a fall
at the party; it burst into life on its own, then switched channels,
picking up static or returning to RCN and the nightly news, a mon-
tage of paramilitaries marching across a field with blackened faces,
and the newsman's lips wiggled as if not his own. Alba lay with her
feet high in the air, supported by the wall, watching those lips and
listening for word of Wilfredo, expecting a photo of his corpse in el
río Bogotá or charred to a twig in a hospital fire. She had gone to el
centro looking for him, and then she stood waiting for Ramón on
la avenida Caracas where a thief reached into her front pockets and
stared at her, daring her to resist, finding nothing except the balled-
up delivery receipts from the fruit counter. She asked Hernán what
he knew, and he told her that Wilfredo had mentioned a dredger
in Quibdó. So then Hernán already knew. At least, she hoped, the
phone would ring. She quit her job to sit next to it.

During those days, Hernán avoided home after school and took
the long route across the lagoon and up la Gran Vía to find la Coca
with her bare feet in the sun of her doorway. Her hands hung between her legs, the way of drunks when their money is spent. He
hugged her. She was not as pretty or warm in his arms as he had
imagined all that morning from his school desk. She smelled gamey,
her neck bent over an orange piece of newspaper from a year ago.

Hers was the blue tank house, a thick-walled cube, sturdy with cemented brick and seeming one of the nicest on la Gran Vía, a thing her father Riki had built with friends when they moved here, but the inside was trashed, full of dirty carpets and broken beds.

"What did you learn today?" she said, her eyes envious of his dark-blue sweater with a torch emblem on his right breast, his geography book in his hand. "And where is Marta?"

He swung his head toward the soccer court across the lagoon. Marta was with Antonio. La Coca reached behind his knee with tenderness and said, "I would like to grow old with you but not here. Maybe Cuturú. Is your house still there?"

He said he didn't know anything about that house. He said it was a bad idea, but he let her talk.

She raised her lip to show her solid teeth. She ran a hand through his hair, cupping his ears and laughing at what she said. Antonio had given her some bright-green jeans, which she had just washed and set out to dry on the street. Pieces of toxic foam, emerging from the drainage of the lagoon, hung from the edges of her house's roof and from the roof of the government day care next door. Lumps of it were being carried by the wind across la Gran Vía. El Progreso had been an unlucky neighborhood, always supporting the wrong politicos in the city council elections of Soacha. This meant the gas line never arrived, their sewage still trickling straight to the lagoon, and no running water. They lacked what had become normal in La Isla and they lacked schools, so just a block over from la Gran Vía, Ramón had sights on constructing his own. It would take at least a year to get the money through Olivia's channels. But Ramón was patient.

"Teach me something or buy us a beer," la Coca said. "What do you want to do? Everything is just so complicated. Have you heard from Wilfredo yet?"

"Nada," Hernán said, avoiding her eyes. "He's a son of a bitch for not calling."

"Sad. Everything is so sad. In this house, in that house. People are fed up. My father is never coming home, or if he is, it will be too late for us."

He opened his geography book to a picture of wave formations; the oceans were stealing the beaches.

"And then what about us?" she said.

"Who? Us?"

"You and I, pendejo. Let's go inside."

They sat on the swirl of wool bedding and water-stained pillows. She had left the door open and through it came the sound of a motorcycle climbing la Gran Vía and women shouting over the sobbing of children at the government day care. He expected them to be interrupted the way young lovers were on television by a mother, a policeman, or even a commercial, and so the viewer often did not know what happened. What happened was that their kissing turned messy. He pressed on the known parts of her, her thighs, her ribs, her shoulders, as if testing her fitness, tooth to gum, eye to socket, and she was complete. She grabbed his hand and made it probe between her legs. How many nights he had imagined what exactly was beneath her jeans? His confusion with the real thing met with her easy knowing.

"Do something new," la Coca said to him. "Do anything."

PART III

The Future

CHAPTER TWENTY-THREE

Quibdó.
Montería.
Santa Marta.
Ibagué.
Cali.

The problem with being displaced was that you could not pick up your life in any other place. You were an interloper, a threat, no matter your story, your accent, always stared at by everyone and usually asked to leave. Only a city would take you, and even there you had to settle among your people or you were not safe.

After a time on a dredger boat in Quibdó, learning to live with the blacks and their music, then pushed around by the paramilitaries on el río Atrato, Wilfredo went north to stay with his brothers on the coast, in hot, crowded houses where if he could not sleep he just had to lay there because the night streets were unsafe, and every chair, couch, patch of floor, carried a human whose dreams he felt he was interrupting with just the tension of his body. These were neighborhoods where paramilitaries put their fingers on everything, a curfew, a storekeeper's ledger, a tax to live anywhere. On a whim, he caught a bus to Boyacá, where he joined a road crew, then took buses south through the mountains, working the harvests, briefly picking coffee, then sorting corn, until he got as far as Cali and slept in the backyard of an abandoned house on el río Cauca.

"Don't come here," Tuts said on the phone. "Caucasia is hot. I sleep with my nail gun. Go back to the capital. They'll forgive you."

"She'll expect something."

"And?"

After a few months of picking fruit at nearby farms, Wilfredo met a woman named Gladis at the market in Cali. She was not looking for a man, just muscle to haul her crop from a farm in the hills outside of Yumbo. He slept cold in a hammock near the barn. He focused on his chores, waking long before sunrise to milk and pull weeds before it got hot, and somehow, in the heat, walking to town every day, his back improved and his head cleared. Working, he did not miss his family as much; they intruded at night in awful dreams with Alba in the panga, Hernán dead in the bow, Milton driving them full speed into the shallows.

Gladis screamed when they had sex, and he would pause above her and think he was raping her. "No!" she screamed loud enough for anyone on the road to hear, for the nearby campesinos to laugh and curse her. It was too much. When they were done, he wondered how it was possible to have landed himself in a new routine. She slept with one leg thrown over his thigh, anchoring herself to him, a farm unsafe, incomplete without a man.

The land belonged to the birds, thousands of them, singing in repetitive and limited melodies every morning and evening. They perched all around him. What did they gather about him? A man always out of place and disbelieving in God but hoping for heaven, a region, he imagined, of open rivers. Nearby ran a creek where he would break apart twigs and watch the current take them down-stream, and, like a child, he imagined they were boats with invisible pangueros and freight being delivered on time. Then he would hear Gladis shouting his name through the trees, needing his service as much as the cows, knocking down bushes with her beloved machete, and sometimes he'd cross the creek to escape her, crawling into the thick green tunnel of undergrowth and laying there still, eyes shut. The birds knew exactly where he was.

In the mornings he and Gladis appeared fresh and new to each other as they crossed paths during their chores, but by late afternoon and evening her face disfigured into a scowl of distrust. She spoke with the whine of a lonely person who misinterpreted half of what he said, for the simple reason that she had gone too long without company. By evening he was sapped of patience and kindness, his words cold and quick, and Gladis acted in a way that made him think she was Alba in a different body, with a full chin, an Alba who had never met him, Alba with luck—a plot of land, some animals, some fruit trees. Like this, he would find Alba in the next town, in another country, and he would be stuck with himself always. He missed her more. She was the original. While other pangueros, being mobile, took advantage of their work to keep cheap lovers in other towns, he had not had anything but a quick screwing of a prostitute in Bagre, a foolish moment, being dragged, as he remembered it, from the cantina to his boat by this strange woman, awaking broke at dawn without his gas tank, which was of much greater value to him than infidelity. His faith was solid and not of great concern to him. His friends joked that he'd rather ride the river than a woman. They took offense at his behavior, certain that he was up to something sick, fucking their wives while posing as Jesús Cristo in the cantina.

The people in the village here were wary of him, too, and the first time he walked the fifteen miles to Yumbo to buy oil and sugar, he was interrogated and held by the military. He told them the truth of his origins, and they laughed at him. They called him a coward. They said his story was pathetic, his wife dishonored. They offered him a radio and said they would pay him to report on the position and numbers of the guerrilleros in the mountains. He had not seen any, he lied.

"None?" they asked, relieved. "Really?"

No wonder they could not win the war.

As paramilitary graffiti accumulated and spilled across walls of schools and stores the closer one got to Yumbo and Cali, their forces approaching, the whole town might soon be considered collaborators of the guerrillas and therefore braced for the sound of that first propane gas bomb. The guerrillas moved wisely about these mountains. El Comandante had the saintly, demented eyes of someone who has been out too long camping and carrying guns; he wore thick teacher glasses and a very old camouflage hat and shook hands with everyone. He acquired books for the village school. He delivered seeds and fertilizer to the farms. Sober and generous, he expected nothing but their respect, their eyes on the road, the woods. He left it clear that the town was theirs to lose or maintain together and that they were safer with him. The only irritating thing, Gladis said, was that you had to laugh at all his jokes, but he was fair for a guerrillero.

"Colombia is rich," el Comandante said once to Wilfredo, summoning him to see his identification card and verify his past, "but our upper class is too selfish. We could bury the guns, the camouflage, the radios, the money. We'd be closer to the people, but"—he snapped fingers—"they'd kill us just like that. They can't suddenly stop hating us after all these years."

Wilfredo told el Comandante his wife was dead, his kids living with their tíos in the capital. He said he had been a farmer near Caucasia, his land his only money, and that was gone. He had no friends, no city skills, only Gladis with her cracked teeth and short hair, her cold reptilian skin.

"Someone has to make her scream," el Comandante said and bought him a beer, then another, making him sit through a long story about a gunfight in which he emerged victorious against a whole battalion of soldiers in Popayán, such a valiant feat that the colonel of the opposing force called him up to congratulate him for his strategy.

On Wilfredo's second trip to Yumbo, where again he reported to the military that he had seen no guerrilleros in those mountains, he was robbed at gunpoint of all the sugar, the rum, the batteries he had bought. He knew he should just keep walking, that Gladis would never believe the most overused story of every poor man to ever drink away his wages.

"Get out!" she said to him when he arrived late with nothing.

He slept in the hammock but in the morning went about his chores.

"Your wife is not dead," she said to the broom she was banging from corner to corner of the one-room shack, swinging the stiff straw hard enough to dig a hole in the floor. He sat at the table eating a bowl of eggs, barefoot, his toenails unclipped and dirty. It was six in the morning, the cows milked already. He had gained weight, and his face was square and dignified. He could break her neck with the broom and bury her in the pasture.

She finished sweeping. She ate a piece of fresh cheese and slapped her hand against the table.

"Entonces?" she said. "Where?"

"In the capital," he said, "with her sister and my son. I don't know what happened to my other son. I'm sure she has found someone else. She's not waiting."

"And here? And my money? Eh? You and your tricks!"

She glared at him across the table, as if he had misunderstood the rules of her invitation months ago and she was just now showing them to him.

"Fine," he said.

He put on his shoes and walked out. Gladis watched him from the back patio as he approached a curve in the road. He turned back once, seeing not her but the mango tree, the familiar birds, the sleepy cows, the hammock. Halfway to Yumbo a truck approached, and he saw it was Calipari, a driver from the village.

"Qué hace, Wilfredo?"

"Where are you going?"

"Tired of the screamer? Get in."

Calipari was a tall man with fashionable black hair, so tall he could not fit into the low-roofed houses of the poor. He had once played basketball for a team in Bogotá but now ran a triangle route with random freight between Cali, Medellín, and the capital. For a time, he said, Wilfredo could serve as his protection and company, though they hardly spoke unless Calipari was falling asleep or it was nighttime in places where if you didn't talk, the road spooked you, roads blocked by guerrilleros, narcos, fallen trees, or with sudden gaps in the pavement. He gave Wilfredo a very small percentage of his earnings, and the money was not so bad because their cargo often came mixed with gasoline tanks or poppy or American whiskey. They kept a .38 revolver inside a hollow Bible on the seat between them. No maps. Calipari knew all the roads and routes, always stopping to hear from other drivers what was ahead, how many police checkpoints, what weather, and like this they avoided hot towns, looking for cold routes and cold people you did not have to bribe.

Despite all Wilfredo's concentration on the gears, the clutch, on the rules of passing and yielding, he did not learn. He found himself too old, too afraid of the velocity, the blind turns. Roads had nothing to do with rivers—no current, no depth, traffic jams everywhere, and rather than break your prop on a shoal, you drove off a cliff or head-on into a bus. Some nights, bored, staring for too long at the yellow center line, Wilfredo saw the swell of a limb detached and thrown into the asphalt. Just a bad memory, he knew, but he would close his eyes and make himself heroic, stabbing el Suizo with his fillet knife or refusing in his doorway, or got even more heroic, taking them downriver—he conjured every bend, island, sunken rock—and jerked the tiller toward his body and watched them fly overboard.

Wilfredo knew Calipari considered him a little stupid, but he had begun to depend on him, not as a friend but as part of his work. In the mornings, high on coffee, they told each other long stories, happy to be in motion, to see the new landscape ahead, and in the afternoons they were quiet, going with the windows down, their eyes dry from coffee, their stomachs full of whatever was cheap. At night, still driving, they tried to imagine an easy place to live where they could stop moving, a trucker hotel or a tourist hotel in the Caribbean, to put both their families in one spot and know their wives were faithful, their children safe. The hotel, they insisted, was the steadiest thing to own and must have a pool, no matter the cost, and they seemed to accelerate toward it—blue water in green tiles, padded reclining chairs, a spring diving board—and took on hotter freight. For driving was a thirsty labor, always waiting in the dust of a police checkpoint while their freight was taken to pieces or having to waste money on bribes, on little bags of water, splurging for fresh coconut water or mango juice. Every day, no matter the hustle, seemed worth any sacrifice to get to that blue pool water.

"Call your wife," Calipari said one night while they were sipping sancocho and it was so hot, the soup, the weather outside of Melgar, that sweat puddled below their elbows on the table. Crickets kept time all over the patio. They were undecided whether to move forward or spend the night in the truck. Calipari rarely sprung for a hotel—they stayed with people he knew—unless they had found women.

Wilfredo carved at an overboiled potato and ate a glob of chicken thigh. A storm was coming, and the truck stop was quiet, the other truckers rushing on to get to the first switchbacks and up the hill to Bogotá before it flooded.

Their destination was Abastos. Wilfredo thought he might see el Chino, and would make sure he unloaded their truck. Once the men from San Andresito had come for the boxes of fancy vodka, which, Calipari said, must taste like pussy on ice, though he'd never tried it—they would look for more freight to get the hell out of the capital before they got robbed or squandered their money at a cantina.

"Alba has moved on," Wilfredo said. "You get up from the bed on one side, and there's another man laying down on the other."

"Maybe. Maybe not."

They sat in the far corner, facing the door, clearly seen by anyone entering. Their bowls had mounds of chicken bones and claws. Two soldiers entered, glanced at them, and ordered beer. These stops were all the same. Rundown, full of staring children, the smell of sun- and rain-ruined objects and human shit. Places to lose money on whores or to pick up more risky freight. Already they had repeated these towns and roads, and Calipari quizzed him about names, streets, the rules of certain markets, and he did not do well.

"She knows you're alive," Calipari said. "Women know. She looks at men similar to you, and she's spiritual so she sees. She hears things you used to say."

"I see her, too."

"Well, good. Without women, we'd still be rubbing clay all over our faces. Carajo! There would be no roads to get to back to them."

They drove fast that night, wide awake. For a while, the salsa they picked up from Bogotá was comforting, but then they switched to RCN, first news of the guerrillero comandante Simón Trinidad being extradited to the United States, and then the families of the kidnapped talking into the station microphone, hoping their beloved were listening in some guerrilla camp. There was an accident ahead. Hundreds of red brake lights rose up the switchbacks to where a semi had lost its brakes and smashed into another. It had been carrying rice bags, burst and spread across the road, and the other was burned down to its skeleton, the indistinguishable freight turned to black pulp and ash. Both drivers had been bagged up, the site

132

marked by flares, and it took the military an hour to shovel the wreckage down to a side road.

It was an example, Calipari said, of why the country remained so poor. They couldn't get things anywhere on time without blowing them up. The guerrillas knocked down all the bridges, and there was just not enough pavement. So they reached Abastos late in the morning, but they did not have to wait as throwers surrounded them and shouted their willingness to carry their weight any distance. Calipari took care of the vodka, while Wilfredo spoke with a seller to get rid of a crate of mangoes and twenty sacks of corn. No sign of el Chino.

"Y?" said Calipari returning. "I got us cargo for Medellín. We have time to kill, hermano, and then we have to rush."

"Ya está," Wilfredo said. "We're done."

"Look." Calipari held up a bottle of vodka and poured some into little cups. It tasted like nothing to Wilfredo, like medicine water.

"You think the rich have all the best things," Calipari said, "but they get as fooled as us sometimes."

Wilfredo looked at a factory outside the fences of Abastos. The women workers wore green frocks, like dentists, and smoked cigarettes. Their hands were red in the gray misty air, their faces, too, and a few leaned over their knees and massaged their own necks.

Most of the trucks were gone, a couple getting loaded for short runs. The cantinas were quiet. They sat in the dark belly of the truck, beneath the black tarp, and finished the bottle of vodka, which had begun to taste better, like liquid potatoes or yucca.

The mist turned to rain, and the women went inside the dark factory. Calipari slept. Watching the puddles fill and then join, the whole lot underwater, Wilfredo saw his mistake. Every day of his other life he had awoken to a river in his doorway, would wade up to his knees at the port and wash his face, taste the yellow water and taste the soil, the rain. It was home. Behind him a little square of earth belonged to him. He should have stood by it. A week ago, he and Calipari had made a run to Montería with a load of motorbikes and looked out at the beef cattle and barbed wire in that humid gloom of green hills. One family owned all of it, Calipari said. Here. There. Straight to the horizon. The valleys, the hills, even the rivers. No one wanted to share.

CHAPTER TWENTY-FOUR

ON THE NUMBERED STREETS of el centro, Alba spent her one day off work from the plastic factory in search of Wilfredo. She put on her best cotton dress with lace borders, a red belt, and red lipstick, sat on the fountains of la avenida Jiménez, smoked Mustang cigarettes, and waited. When she saw him, and he saw her, he would wake up to his error and come home. His story would be logical enough to accept.

Te quiero, he would say, and she would say it back. She would interrupt his apology and say it did not matter. She wanted him with her and she had a job now, so if they were very careful, they could get by.

Sometimes she called Tuts who still claimed to know nothing beyond Wilfredo's failed stint on a dredger in Quibdó.

Is he alive? she said.

Yes, Tuts said.

When Alba returned home, the phone rang. In the divisions of a second, a full day's hope blossomed into theories: Wilfredo was on a boat in el Chocó, too far from phones and roads, or he was on a construction crew on the road to Tunja, a foreman in a brick factory in Sesaima.

"Hola, mi amor," she said. "Wilfredo?"

"Milton, por favor," the woman said in a throaty Caribbean voice.

"He doesn't live here. He's in el centro. Are you Lucila? I am Alba."

"Tell him suerte. Tell him when you see him. Suerte que le digo."

"What do you mean?"

Luck? Everything was out of place in time, in her heart, and she decided she may as well wash her face and go to sleep. She had simply spent too much of her life fretting over her dead babies and lost husband. What about her live sons? Six months ago, Hernán, sixteen years old and tall enough to bend down for people, his upper lip browned by what was almost a mustache, had not come home. Then there was this ugly girl with a cut on her cheek, mi novia, he said in a low hoarse voice, la Coca, mamá, and she scratched her armpits like a dog and sat on the couch without asking permission. Pregnant now, and Hernán only visited to borrow money. Worse, a year ago, Alba had opened the door at dawn, and Milton was squatting there.

How did you find the house? she had said.

I can find anyone.

He had more tattoos, reddish birds, a Colombian flag, a pistol, a vulture with a woman's legs. He had circular white scars and pink burns on his muscular arms.

I served, he said. I'm done.

His face was like el Suizo's. She hated the look of him. His milky eyes, his grinned-up mouth, a malignancy in his lack of breathing. He was supposed to sleep near her on the still unfinished floor of the living room, but he remained awake and circling, smoking her Mustangs, rubbing his head where the hair was growing back around a thick noodle of scar tissue.

He's dangerous, Ramón had said. I want him to leave.

He came to see *me,* Alba said.

You can't see what's there.

No? Where do I come from then? I know his look.

To Milton she said, We don't agree with your choices, mi amor. You have to calm down if you want to stay with us. You have to work.

Milton tried to learn Hernán's algebra, listening to explanations for $2x - 2 = 0$. He wanted to do good. He brought home religious pamphlets: *Jesús wants you inside him. Let Jesús inside you.* He tried to help at La Esperanza, but the children recognized his look, his kindness unsteady before he fell apart and hurt them. His carpentry skills were gone, poof, into whatever happened in the jungle. He talked about poking the eyes of dead people to see if they would jump, to avoid having them shoot him in the back. He talked about his rifle, María Talía, whom he loved and still joked with sometimes. He asked Hernán for the names of his enemies in the neighborhood and offered to kill them.

Olivia came in her blue vest and made Milton fill out paperwork to join a work and therapy program for ex-combatants. He told his story: they had picked him up three years ago outside of Caucasia and took him for basic training in Puerto Boyacá, then stationed him near Barrancabermeja to protect the oil refinery. A fellow soldier, one who always had money for hookers and rum and pot, asked him to help with some night work. They could go after anyone they wanted rather than just stand there guarding a bridge. He got his release from the military.

Paid based on merit, Olivia said.

Exactly, Milton said. Exactly.

Did you cut up bodies? she said.

We did the worst.

For whom?

For those who got the big promotions. The ones you see on television.

She's a guerrillera, Milton said later at dinner. I just signed my death sentence.

No, no, Olivia was good, Alba explained. She paid for Hernán's school. She found her work at the plastic factory. She cared.

Listen, Ramón said. They had sat there with a bottle of Néctar aguardiente, a knife with some blood on it where Lidia had dug a sliver out of her thumb and cut herself badly. They were drunk on no occasion, feeling vicious and hungry, like rats or water moccasins in the low light of the dangling bulb that had turned brown somehow, as if full of water and covering them in a sandy texture.

Listen, Ramón said again. You have to leave now. When these people come to get you, they won't look much at faces. They'll take us all out.

True, Milton said. True.

When he left, Alba thought he would end up in the lagoon or running one of the death squads at the top of the hill, but just a day later the phone rang and it was him to tell her he found work as a security guard in northern Bogotá. He would be guarding the rich and their assets, he said, no different than being in the jungle but here it was cleaner with fewer snakes. I love you, she had told him. I want you to be good again.

"Tía, are you hallucinating?" said Marta who was extremely pregnant with flakes of pastry on her chin. She stood in a bare area of the floor where the mosaic tiles had never been laid and somehow got lost or broken over the years. "Wake up. Hernán is here with his novia, and I don't want to see them."

"I know," Alba said. "He wants money. Is it the baby that bothers you? Estás bien? Your face is a little green."

"It's every whore on this hill," Marta said. "If they could leave me in peace, I would rest. Alone. All I want is silence."

"It would be hard," Alba said, "except no one would talk to you. You'd talk to yourself like I do."

La Coca's stomach was not as big as Marta's, but it was swollen, and Alba touched it continuously, giving her weird countryside advice for her diet. Hernán ran upstairs to hug Lidia who lay sick in bed with her cut finger. La Coca needed to see a doctor, he said, and Alba gave them all of her money minus her bus fare for the week. She told him about Milton's job. He was decent and moral again. When would they go visit him? Hernán kissed her cheek and rubbed her shoulders to thank her. He said they would go soon on her day off, but not this week or the next, because the neighborhood was not safe at night. There were rumors she shouldn't worry about. He had been connected with doings of the gang in el Progreso. El Progreso? Alba shook her head. It was a good moment, but then Marta, so fickle in those days, walked in with a bowl of rice and pinched a lump of salt onto her tongue and called la Coca a dirty puta.

"Stop," Alba said, as the girls crashed, la Coca striking with her nails and Marta biting into the back of her neck. They were too weak to do much damage, but la Coca had blood on her back. Hernán grabbed la Coca, and Alba pulled Marta down onto a chair and held her in her lap. She looked strangely relaxed, her legs up in the air, half-naked in her underwear, and you could see her breath in the cold air and a thousand little white bumps on the skin of her stomach. Marta's belly was massive, even as she lay on her back, and what would happen to all her intelligence? I have more, the hot eyes said. I'm not afraid of the world.

"I'm not sorry," la Coca said.

"What?" Marta said. "I'll kill you, puta."

It was in everyone. Pride, a hard bright pearl in a filthy shell.

I will rot without a man soon, Alba thought. That's what this is about. But who?

"I have to sleep," Alba said. "We need to clean this up."

"She leaves!" Marta said.

"Vamos," Hernán said.

"I hope I trip and fall on your corpse," la Coca said.

"Stay," Alba said, but no one listened to her, and it seemed like one more day off down the drain.

CHAPTER TWENTY-FIVE

IN THE CANTINA the men drank hard, thumbing back the labels of their beers and examining with wishful eyes the unlit disco ball, the sticky floor, and imagined it all of some value, as if marble, a palace in the hills. Being this drunk was perplexing. They added to the feeling, one beer over another, until the reward of their day's labor went from a brief euphoria to an urge to piss all over the floor and break someone's eye sockets with a fist.

Hernán watched them. He sat across the street on the steps of the government day care and considered the double doors of the two-story emerald-green structure, too nice a cantina for el Progreso. He focused on Ramón who was establishing an alibi among the drunks. Ramón danced with the only woman present, who, unlike Lidia, was skinny to an extreme, braless so that her breasts pointed sideways, her massive eyes divided by a statuesque, beautiful nose. The men scowled a little, not because they cared to dance with her but because they wanted Ramón to buy them a final round. They knew some of his secrets. They had supported the construction of his new school, would hand out free tamales when he ran for the city council in Soacha, and would stand up for him at the neighborhood meetings, even if he was from up over the hill, not one of them. They were still thirsty.

Water stood everywhere mirroring the streetlamps. Still no aqueduct in el Progreso, and the night before the neighborhood had experienced a deluge of water delivery in a sudden overkill act of service from the Bogotá water department. After Hernán filled their tanks to the brim, then bathing himself and la Coca, filling every pot and water bottle, even spraying the sides of the house, the floor, he pointed the hose into the night and watched it flow down the alley into a stream to the lagoon.

Hernán took a turn around the block and neared la Coca's old house. Her father Riki had made his dreamed-of return, but far too late. La Coca was too old for the local schools. Riki's turquoise Ford shined arrogantly below the streetlight, the black tarp open on the trailer to show there was no freight to steal. No one in the family had recognized him after five years, and he was treated like a gay clown by his three daughters, shunned by his wife who wanted only the money and his departure so her lover could return to her bed.

Hernán circled back to the cantina where the volume had spiked in his absence. Late, but they had a right to this noise—cowbell, trumpet, the bragging voice of Johnny Rivera who sang it was better to be single, more fun, but no one cared, the CD scratched, and the men sagging almost to the floor. Hernán heard someone say his name and in his distraction had no idea where it came from or if he had imagined it.

"What's my problem?" he whispered, sitting on the stoop of the government day care. "These fucked people."

"What's your problem?" said a voice behind him. There was no one under the streetlamps but him. "Too smart."

"Antonio?"

A cigarette burned in the dark hood. Antonio crouched at the stoop, and the two inspected each other in their black outfits. Silver glinted on Antonio's finger, and a pair of sunglasses covered his eyes.

"A little dark for those glasses," Hernán said.

"Everything, Pollito," Antonio said, "I see everything."

Hernán tried to make a hard fist with his hand, watching Ramón twirl the woman, letting himself get twirled, grinning at the other men. He had the money now, his tailor shop expanded, his school just up the street.

Stay, la Coca had said to Hernán less than an hour ago, combing her hair into the sink. It's easy, Hernán told her. This will give us something, and I can find something else in Bogotá, something better. He was good, almost a man, for saying a thing like that, but it was hard to mean anything when the baby was making weight, blood and bone, trying to get comfortable in the womb just like them in their lumpy bed and leaky house.

"You have to respect Ramón," Antonio said. "He built himself from nothing, and he's always looking for something new. He does some good."

"He's a son of a bitch," Hernán said.

"He's family."

"No. La Coca."

"She's a woman."

"And?"

"Forget it. I'm armed. You should know. Let's go."

*

Ramón had wanted bricks, but too many people were scamming between him and the Bogotá donors, and so his school was made of cheap shit, three boxes of matchstick wood on stilts, the thin blond planks glowing for that first week in the sun, the type of structure to crumble from termites within a few years. All day, children swarmed in their blue sweaters, and it was real to them, a thing to put hope up against, despite the odds. Ramón officially called it La Idea, the community's school, but everyone knew it was just business, that he was positioning himself for another run at the city council in Soacha. No one knew where the money came from—as tailors were humble people—but assumed that Ramón had the gift of all gangsters, which was to turn cheap things like thread and cloth or now

142

desks, books, paper, pencils into a front for something valuable.

Hernán tightened his hood and worked his way up a muddy rut. His heart seemed to be pumping air, not blood, into his chest, and his legs seemed pressurized from it, potent, as he easily scaled the locked wooden door behind Antonio. Two classrooms faced each other, a padlocked office tacked to the edge of one, and at the rear was the third classroom with the library. Both of them smeared their footprints across the muddy patio. Two quick slashes with the sharpened screwdriver, and Antonio tore the tiny padlock free from the door. An entire wall was filled with books, some shelved out of reach, others in high piles. Antonio lit a match to spark a small white candle, raised his sunglasses, and scanned the spines. The selection was random with books by Cervantes, Verne, Dostoevsky, books on architecture, books on engine repair, books with pictures of rainforest frogs and snakes. High up, in perfect order, they spotted the golden letters on maroon-and-khaki-colored spines of the new complete set of Encyclopedias Británicas. Their objective. They worked fast, stacking the books inside garbage bags set atop the children's desks. Antonio disappeared briefly to the other classroom and returned with something in his pockets.

"Stop," Antonio said, blowing out the candle.

A nearby television mumbled about a new shampoo for women wanting straighter hair, this accompanied by a radio commercial dialogue of a girl asking if she could possibly learn English even if she did not have blue eyes. "Sí, señora!" said a man's voice. "Anyone can learn at Instituto Lengua Americana!" The drainage of the lagoon gurgled a hundred feet off the ledge. Hernán pushed a ball of spit around his mouth. If the patrol were to step into the patio of the school, the accumulating air in his chest and legs might explode. Never hide, Antonio had taught him, never go home. Run down the hill to la Autopista Sur. Distance will save you. If they get close, you zigzag because these pendejos can't shoot anything.

Hernán imagined himself laid out on a desk, doodled upon and picked at by blades.

No wind. The boards of the wooden boxes creaked. Perhaps it was just the termites in hysterical labor or a rat breaking into Ramón's office to devour the United Nations snacks. Through the dark, he could see the form of Antonio's revolver against his hand.

"Tranquilo," Antonio said, tapping his bad ear, the one, he said, which had gone deaf one day while he was fucking Caterín. He put his cold, mud-crusted hand on Hernán's wrist. "Let's avoid the lagoon. We'll walk the alleys, a straight shot. It's better."

"What did you hear?"

"Breathe, Pollito. We're fine."

*

The moon was high overhead, white. In their dark clothes, they seemed powdered with chalk. Though darker, usually unpatrolled, the alleys were louder with the excess water and ran flush against the thin walls where sleeping heads rested. They focused on each step, the bags heavy, cradled in both arms. The puddles were of unclear depths, and the stinky mud might sink an inch or a foot, sending you crashing into a thin wall. They heard the whistling sound of water still leaking from a hose into an overflowed tank.

On the corner of la Gran Via, two blocks uphill from the cantina and the day care, Antonio grabbed Hernán's arm. He could see on the stoop of the day care two men of the patrol, rifles slung over their necks, their faces concealed by hoods.

Drop the bag, Hernán thought. La Coca will open the door, fish out her underwear from the foot of the bed, the green pair with the little white stars woven in, always a smell of burned hair in the elastic, too tight for her expanding hips, ringing them with purple ridges.

Antonio held up a finger.

"Tranquilo," he whispered, watching the men through his sunglasses.

It had not been tranquilo for the pretty boy who had been shot a dozen times, laid out for his mother to find him on the cement washing table in Villa Esperanza. A night messenger, he had called himself, a guide to any pendejo arriving home late from el centro or needing to see a girlfriend or sick brother. For a price he took people down or up over the hill. He was high up in heaven now, no darkness there, so he probably was not very happy.

"Look," Antonio whispered. One hood sat down to smoke while the other talked on his phone. "Take off your shoes." A long pool of water reflected pure white across la Gran Vía.

They waited for one of the men to look away, as he put out his cigarette, but before that the moon merged into a thin cloud, and he turned to it, tapping the other's shoulder. Likely born in the countryside, they could not help looking.

Antonio ran briefly through the light, and in a few strides they had both crossed the street, splashing loudly into the next pool. They glided through another streetlamp after another block, and in the darkness beyond it Antonio slipped and crashed into the side of a house.

The spooky sound of a baby crying emerged from a near wall. A melodious tapping accompanied it, perhaps a hammer searching a wall for studs, and the whole house trembled.

"Dios," Antonio said. Stiff hair stuck out his hood, his mouth open. He plucked his sunglasses off his head.

The tapping ceased, and a man shrieked, "Who's out there? Eh? Ladrones, carajo! Ladrones! Auxilio! Hijos de putas!"

A light came on and the neighborhood was awake.

CHAPTER TWENTY-SIX

ANTONIO BOLTED THE DOOR shut, and they searched the empty house, the bathroom, the back patio. They lay flat on their backs, fists pressed into the concrete floor. A dog was howling, exciting other dogs.

The living room and kitchen walls were lined with uncomfortable wooden and metal chairs where no one gathered. Underneath the chairs were magazines, Bibles, bricks, buckets, and what used to be a long oval mirror, broken and hung there beside a blue-eyed Jesús Cristo holding up his bleeding hands, beneath him the words *Follow me.* The table, perhaps at some point the wall of someone's house, was a long, shapeless piece of plywood with splintered edges. It sagged under the weight of both the encyclopedias and an unplugged television with a curling crack across its screen.

Antonio lit a cigarette, handed it to Hernán, the smoke harsh to his dry throat. They stayed put a few minutes, watching the smoke float up into the rusty corrugations of the roof, until Antonio screwed in a dim lightbulb to an exposed wire and pulled the books from their bags, setting the pistol on the table within reach. He licked his black tooth, his face pink and dripping, and a blue vein expanded across his forehead. From the deep pockets of his sweatshirt he pulled out two light sockets, a bent up stretch of copper wiring, and a rubber-banded bundle of long screws with sharp points. "Something extra for us. Do you two need any of this?"

"Stupid," Hernán said.

"Let's have a look." Antonio opened letter *I* of the encyclopedias. The glossy pages shined with colored maps and photos in the perfect order of all that had been thought and lived and existed on earth. The paper smelled sour and the gilt-edges dazzled in the dim light, making you want to turn them. Antonio was eying a photo of rust-colored earth striped with rows of green olive trees. He turned the page to the square head and thrust-out chest of Mussolini. He sniffed the hard glue of the binding, set it on the table, and ran his fingers over the lettering. "Imagine just picking an olive off a tree and eating it. Look here. Mussolini. So they loved him and then they hung his dead body from a meat hook and threw rocks at it. That's something we would do, no?"

Hernán, yet to open a book, pulled back a potato-sack curtain near the sink, snagged it on a nail to keep it drawn. There was a small light on the horizon. The night was much longer when you were awake in it.

"You're in no hurry," Antonio said. "Now, there's only one way to do this. We read *A* to *Z* without exceptions. When do you take the test for the university?"

"In a month, in Bogotá."

"Are you ready?"

"I don't know. If Cate did well . . . I know as much as her. Are you my tutor now?"

"The only person who knows more than these books is God," Antonio pronounced. He put down *I* for Italy and flipped through *A,* licking the popped blood vessels on his lips, and Hernán longed to punch out his black tooth and slap his deaf ear. La Coca was right. There was a thing in Antonio you could not talk to or understand. He was unhooked by his random, sudden beliefs, a cataclysm of action to follow, thinking now he was at the center of things, nodding his head as if awakened to his calling. A learner.

Hernán opened letter *C* reluctantly. Encyclopedic Colombia was all coffee trees, a woman with a plug of tobacco smoking in her lips, her apron laden with red beans. General Santander next to the flag. Red buses in Bogotá. Oil wells smoking. Hearts of palm. Bananas. So much was missing.

A gunshot stopped Antonio's page-turning, followed by another long fit of barking across the hill.

"A strange time for it," Antonio said. "Why don't you look at *B* and go in order? Eh?"

"What's the point? These aren't ours."

"Forget the plan, Pollito. We are keeping them now. I had no idea they were so valuable."

The plan? It was that Ramón would be at La Idea in the morning, opening doors for the children in blue sweaters, and then, drawing equations and maps on the whiteboard, would find some reason to consult the encyclopedias and yell to the children, "Ladrones! Ladrones!" It would not be the first time. During the construction of the school, Ramón had felt underappreciated, unremunerated by the churches and vests who donated materials, and so he stole from himself. He hired every thief in the neighborhood to slip in there at night and snatch tools, bags of cement, books, a computer, even a load of wood, all of which, for a fee, they would return to him on a corner in Soacha so he could sell them, stealing so much that the neighbors gathered money to make sure the patrol lingered there most of the night.

"What are you going to tell Ramón then?" Hernán said. "He's going to announce this. He probably already spent the money he expects to get for them."

"He'll have to understand, parce. He's not from this side of the hill. I am."

Maybe it was true. The clock ticked on Ramón, who would have been safer as just a tailor. Someday, they would find his body on the corner, but for now he was the one connection with the capital beyond the hill, with the corporations, the politicos, and the priests, and the neighbors were afraid to lose it, no matter how many times he fed their hopes for a new giant antenna for their televisions, a park, a network of sewage pipes for their shit, and came through with nothing. Who else could get a visit from the U.S. ambassador, serve her agua panela, and discuss his dream of skating on a frozen pond in America? This while the American soldiers and snipers fell through thin roofs on la Gran Vía, and all the hotheads who said they hated the United States, hated Spain, got excited at the first glimpse of her SUVs, thinking the ambassador might open a suitcase with jobs in Miami, drop pavement on the streets, maybe drain the lagoon for a park. Who knows? they said. She's here.

They both read for quite a while in silence, forgetting the time. Hernán flipped fast through various letters, pausing at some of the more beautiful and ambiguous pictures, which, it was true, gave him something like hope.

"Let's count them," Antonio said, stacking the books in alphabetical piles.

Antonio could do some things well, scare a bigger man with a knife to give up his wallet, dig deep holes into rock-hard earth for a house, throw crates all day at Abastos, fuck and fuck and fuck, they said, his dick never soft, but not this, not turning new words into a real job at an office or a clinic or a refinery. Hernán refused to believe in the books, but he might take one with him, a hostage.

"La puta mierda!" Antonio said. "We are missing *L* and one of the *M*s. Do you see them?" He stomped around the table in his wet socks, lighting a match close to the golden letters to be sure. "What starts with those letters? Something good. Mierda! I bet they're out there in the alley somewhere. My bag ripped."

"Ramón won't know the difference. We sell him these, get our cut, and forget about it. Then you could fix your teeth."

149

"My teeth?"

"If we left a trail of books, people are going to talk, even your mamá. When does she get back?"

"You don't get it. I'll pay you my part. Take my television." He sat down and opened *F* to Francia. "What do you know, Pollito? Who was Napoleón Bonaparte?" He closed the book over one finger and pressed it against his chest. "Well?"

"He was French, a general."

"What did he do?"

"He invaded countries, fought wars. What do I know? He killed pendejos."

"Which ones?"

"Russia, I know. Spain."

"Why are you stuck on this hill, Pollito? You never taught me anything." He lit a cigarette and squinted across the table. "When I'm done with all these, I won't be too proud to share what I know. You may need it and all you'll have is a television and maybe la Coca who will be ugly as shit in a few years and then you'll call me Napoleón."

Hernán's feet were wet, numb. The rising sun was blocked by the hill, but he could see it lighting up the neighborhoods across the lagoon. He heard footsteps of neighbors leaving for work in the city.

"I'm leaving," Hernán said, shoving the letter *T* into his belt and under his shirt. "I'll be by this afternoon. We'll go see Ramón."

Antonio shook his head, his finger pressed into the face of Henry Ford, then a picture of an assembly line, unable to hold back his smile at this phenomenon. "Not me."

"Then I'm taking the television."

"Take it."

*

The day was bright. As soon as Hernán stepped out into the sun, he regretted the television in his hands. He heard the bolt shut on the door—Antonio back to the table, holding one eye close to the glossy pages where his warty finger traced print, not even comprehending anymore, but mouthing the words, expecting them to join, not just in his ejaculating brain, but in his heart where he would make decisions to convert the new sweat of education into a way to end his days of throwing crates at Abastos and robbing pendejos in San Mateo. Poorer one television and the money Ramón would have paid him, the leader, Napoleón, saw new angles, new answers to old questions. He might kill the tedium, which was killing them all.

Shoveling clay into the foundation of a two-story brick house, two men paused to squint at Hernán. He tried to step casually past them but the television was awkward, all its weight in the glass screen; it cut the flow of blood to his fingers and slid the letter *T*—a gift for la Coca—gradually down his jeans. Did they notice? Even in a glance, people of the hill perceived the contents of your pockets— a payday, a knife, a chocolate bar for your novia.

At the corner of la Gran Vía, he turned uphill. In the government day care, the babies screamed and rattled their toys.

"Shut up!" the day care women yelled. "Shut up!"

He looked around at the quiet houses. The cantina was locked with a steel curtain over the entrance. The night was gone and so was its mystery, just shacks and paths. Just home. He blinked. The sun left the hill naked, worse than humble. The wind sent plastic bags end-over-end against the walls. Some antennas swayed. Clothes clipped to lines on roofs fluttered.

He walked along the far wooden barrier of La Idea, the air seeping back into his gut. Blue-sweatered children ran crazy circles around the schoolyard, tackling one another and lodging their heads between small gaps of the fence to peer out.

"Hola, Pollito," one boy yelled, triggering a chorus of red-cheeked boys and girls with hungry, bright eyes.

"Hola, Pollito," they all yelled. "Nice television! Does it work? Eh, Pollito?"

He tried for the top of the hill, but he couldn't make it. He dumped the television on the stoop of an abandoned shack and noticed his crouched prints from the night before, turning from shoes to feet. They needed rain to wash away the prints, but the sky was all blue with spotty clouds on the horizon. He adjusted the book in his sweatshirt and looked down the alley for the shine of a dropped encyclopedia.

"Hernáncito!" Ramón came up behind him, like death, gray-faced, blood-eyed from his hangover.

"Buenos días," Hernán said.

"Where did you get that television? Does it work?"

"I don't know."

Ramón talked in a way that meant this was all theater for el Progreso, for any neighbor who could hear. He carried two full plastic bags of UN cookies and yogurt for the children.

"They robbed us," Ramón said. "Last night. I went to open the school today and no light sockets, no wiring, so I investigated. They took the new set of encyclopedias, not from me, hermano, but from the children. From all of us! Can you believe it?"

"I'll ask around," he said. "Do you have any eggs?"

"Eggs? You used to dig holes," Ramón said, lowering his voice. "Remember? Hah! You should do that again and put your friend in one."

"I have to go."

"Maybe it's the static in my mind," Ramón whispered, "but who asked you to take away the light sockets? Eh? Imagine these kids trying to read in the dark. It's unfair. And what kind of idea is it walking around with a television. Eh? Leave it here. How much attention do you want?"

"Talk to Antonio. I'm done with it."

"What else did you take? Eh?"

"Talk to Antonio."

"I'm talking to you. I have no eggs. Do you want yogurt?"

"No."

"It's a privilege doing business with me. Realize it. When I'm elected to the council in Soacha, I'll need your help."

They were interrupted by a group of girls in flannel skirts and white socks, on their way downhill to the causeway across the lagoon to Hernán's school. Marta was among them, her blue sweater stretched out by the hump of her growing baby. She carried it as if it were nothing. Her hair grew in two bleached-blond streams behind her ears, the dark roots like a rotten specks in a piece of fruit. She still hoped to ace the standardized tests and go to the university.

"Hola, papá," Marta said. "Hola, primo."

"Hola, Pollito," the girls said, stepping around a pile of foam. "You're late. Are you coming? Nice television."

"I'm sick," he said. "I'll be back tomorrow."

"Sick? We'll miss you. Get better."

The girls seemed to use only their hips to keep their legs in motion. They kicked dust into the light, and the wind threw their hair above their heads. Ramón leaned forward, his forehead glittering with sweat, and focused his bloodshot eyes on all the butts, even that of his daughter. He sniffed the air. The cantina owner raised his steel curtain, sweeping and grinning. One of the day care women stepped out, screaming once through the door before she kicked it closed, and looked sharply at the girls, as if they were walking straight out of the slum and into paradise.

Hernán picked up the television.

"Help me on this," Ramón said, rubbing his eyes with a piece of his shirt. "Don't be stupid or it will go bad for all of us. OK?"

CHAPTER TWENTY-SEVEN

NO EGGS OR MILK. The cell phone blinked green in its charger. The wool blankets smelled like Hernán's sweat. La Coca lay between the dips in the bed, jabbing her fingers into different parts of her belly. The time had passed, Caterín said, when they could shove a vacuum inside you. Her cousin, a hooker in Chicó, had gotten rid of a half-dozen babies, her only complaint that the nurses were spooky, for who chose a job like that? Who chose any job? la Coca wondered.

When he comes, la Coca thought, watching the sky go blue in the skylight, I won't say a word. We can stare and disapprove.

She pulled her underwear up with her toes and raised her knees to get it around her ankles, cold air leaking in from the sides like water. She hurried into a warm sweatshirt and jeans, as if a whole tepid, deflated body had been stored down there. She kicked out her legs and stood up on the hard dirt floor.

I am better than this, she thought.

A bag of concrete powder leaned in the corner.

Soon, Hernán had said. Antonio would help, and they'd lay the floor and sand it smooth.

Why this pendejo, her father Riki had said, home from the coast, when it was too late. Hernán had no trade, no skills. He was useless. A woman was always ceding, her mother added, mashing plantains for frying, a welcome dinner of patacones, roasted chicken, and beer. Learn to. It was what one did. Don't even pay attention if he changes.

La Coca drank two mugs of the fresh water, lit the stove with a match, then opened a little bag of coffee to find less than a table-spoon. She dipped her wet finger in and sucked off the grains, dipping again until it was gone, and closed the valve of gas to the stove.

"Listo," she said.

You were meant for better, Riki had told her, a piece of chicken falling from his mouth. Her pendejo would be dead in a year.

How would you know? she said.

He knows.

But first he'll get you pregnant, her mother said. Visualize that type of life. It will all be my fault. I was not watchful.

La Coca sat on an overturned bucket outside the door and hugged her belly. She shut her eyes. Here the dirt was soft on her feet, and she pressed her toes into it, like a campesina, she thought. It was the gunshots that had awoken her. She remembered now. She looked out over the patchwork roofs for the black flies, the curious crowd. All was calm. The puddles were bright in the sun, and the neighbors splashed right through them on their way to work.

Stay, she had said.

She put on the blue Comcel vest, the cell phone in her pocket, and returned to the cement block where she dipped a pair of blue jeans into a bucket of water, scrubbing with a round soaped rock. The water turned bluish. Already her bad shoulder clicked, her elbow burned, and she almost choked on her tongue at the realization that the sun was this high and no Hernán.

She loved water as much as he, to sip it in bed, no matter how cold. It all came from the sky or from a tank in Bogotá. It would all run out, Riki said, even if the pendejo lives.

Go, she told herself, her stomach asking for it. Go to the corner and work. Sell three calls and eat.

When she was ten, Riki had come home in his red truck all the way from Cartagena and took her the same day, just her, to the indoor pool in Bogotá. The water was green in dirty yellow tiles men grabbed hold of to rest between laps, ten lanes splashing, echoing up to the vaulted ceiling. Riki loved laps, all alone in his lane, his arms reaching up high, as if for fruit, then dropping hard into the water. He held her away from his body and helped her glide along the surface.

He tricked her. He let her go. She swallowed water until her toes touched the tiles. When she hit the surface, Riki grabbed her armpits and kissed her on the lips.

A survivor! He said over the din of swimming.

Her head was loud, her own breathing echoing off the ceiling, her lungs in charge of her body, wanting it to live.

The locker room was all rusty lockers and naked men who did not look at her. If they looked, Riki would kill. She felt drunk on the steamy smells of hot urine, chlorine, cologne, and cigarette smoke. She watched the foam of shampoo spinning in the hair-clogged drains. A survivor, she toweled off and waited on a wooden bench while Riki entered a stall with another man. She shivered and waited, trying to put on her socks and comb her hair.

When she opened her eyes to hang up the socks, it was as if someone had slapped a white lens across her eyes and Hernán stood directly in front of her, setting down Antonio's television. He reached for her armpits, pulling her up into the air. She felt something hard, flat against her belly.

"Look what I brought," Hernán said.

She touched the cracked screen, the busted dial where one would have to use pliers to change the channels.

"I'm leaving," she said. "It's not a joke. Don't smile."

"Look." He tilted his head, still gripping her arm.

"I saw it already," she said.

He stuck his other hand under her sweatshirt, rolling down the tight cotton of her underwear and caressing the ring of purple ridges on her waist.

"And food?" she said. "There's no milk or eggs. Just a block of raw sugar and water and I'll vomit if I drink more of that."

He unzipped his black hooded sweatshirt and pushed it into the water of the bucket, then pulled an encyclopedia from his pants.

"For you," he said.

Bringing things was his way. He brought her the plastic for the skylight, the cinnamon candles they lit at night, and chocolate bars to eat with coffee.

He dragged her inside, grabbed her from behind, trying to work his fingers through the loopholes of her jeans. He was trying to pull her onto the bed.

"Antonio went crazy," he said. "He's a scholar now."

He pinched the waistband of her underwear again and crouched down to look at the stretched fabric.

"Stop," she said.

"I just wanted to see it."

"I'm so hungry," she said.

"I'll make something."

"What?"

He went onto the patio, where he struggled to pick up the television and set it down inside out of the light. They lay together on the mattress. Soon her stomach would start again. She would have to break into her mother's house and see what food they could take without seeming desperate.

"Were you with another?" she said.

"Do I smell like another?"

"Tell me," she said. "Tell me or I leave."

"I was with Antonio. We robbed the encyclopedias from La Idea."

"No one saw?"

"No one saw."

"I saw you. I saw everything. Do you realize? What about school?"

"I'm tired, mi amor. Let me rest a little, then we'll talk slow. Then you can tell me what you know."

She made a random hang-up call to check whether the cell phone was still working: "Aló," said the voice of a bogotano, un rico perhaps.

"There's business," she said. "Me voy."

"Bring money," he said. "I love you."

She kissed Hernán's open lips, and he breathed on her face, asleep. She could blow him or drip cold water on his forehead, drag him out into the muddy patio, and he would just keep sleeping like nothing. She wrapped the encyclopedia in two plastic bags and filled a plastic bottle with water, and in a few minutes she was walking past La Idea, the causeway, down through the worsening shacks of Villa Esperanza, past the washing women, and off the hill toward Soacha.

In a dirt parking lot, a makeshift terminal for city buses, a driver stood on his hood, scrubbing the windshield with a sponge. "Just wait a moment, nena," he yelled, "and I'll take you wherever." He licked his fingers and stuck them down his pants. "Ay, qué empanadota!" She walked faster. Antonio would kill him for this, she thought, but would Hernán?

Five minutes later, she walked down the main street of San Mateo, through the redbrick ravine, a jam of buses, people loitering at the corners, the encyclopedia sweating in her hand. She looked up at the blackened windows of a discotheque where she had once mourned for her dead novio, her first love, and was unfaithful to him. She drank from the water bottle, filling her belly with nothing. The baby would remember this day.

"Llamadas!" she yelled, though she was not yet to her corner. "Llamadas! Llamadas!"

"Muchacha," a man said, a black leech of blood under his eye. "A cuánto?"

"Three-hundred pesos." She handed him the phone and listened to him tell his novia he was not coming, he had been robbed, and he was so sorry. A lie. Yes, he loved her. Why didn't she understand? He was on a corner with no money. He was hurt. "You don't need me? Fine." He hung up.

"Nine-hundred pesos," la Coca said, and he paid.

After an hour on a bench by la Autopista Sur, only three calls sold, she flipped through the luminous pages of *T,* which made a tearing sound as they had never been turned. She stuck her finger into the black funnel of a Tornado, the white breast of a Tennis player, and into the golden crown of the queen of Thailand who was pretty as a doll.

"How much for the book?" said another seller with an open grill of bright red sausages and toasted arepas.

"Why sell it?" she said. "It's part of a complete set."

"For my son," he said. "It's his birthday next week, and he studies at Camilo Torres in el centro. Tell me what it's worth, and I'll bring you the money tomorrow."

"You can start with a sausage, make it hot."

He heated a fat red link, turning the valve of the propane on his grill, and everything sizzled. She could feel it in her spine.

"A la órden," he said, serving it to her wrapped in a buttered arepa.

She bit into the toasted corn shell and tough skin of the meat with a shock and felt the blood and hot grease shoot down her throat. She ate so fast she swallowed the fat without chewing it, and her throat ached as the large bites squeezed into her chest. She asked for another.

"A nice girl like you . . ." he said. He had what seemed like kindness in his voice, but his eyes were cold. " . . . should not be on the corner to start. You should meet my son, Juan. We are humble, but we think about the future. That's the problem up there." He pointed at the hill. "No strategy."

"How much?" she said.

"For the book?"

"No, the arepa."

"For you, free."

His eyes wandered the edges of her body. All was sex with the bored sellers and all the men she had ever known, with nothing to do but imagine themselves fucking you, dead or alive. The clouds were closing around the sun, and she looked at it, knowing she might not see it for weeks. She held the book tight against the side of her belly.

"Llamadas!" she screamed. "Llamadas! Llamadas!"

CHAPTER TWENTY-EIGHT

ON THEIR WAY to a community meeting in el Progreso, an older man and woman, both storeowners, stumbled upon *L* and *M,* lodged into a little gutter just beyond the crossing of la Gran Vía. They had gotten word about the robbery of La Idea, and they followed the footprints to Antonio's door and interrupted him as he was in the process of burying half the set in his back patio.

He told them the best truth. Why shouldn't he? He acted alone, he said, but under Ramón's direction. And Antonio belonged to them, to el Progreso—one of the first to arrive at the hill when there was no water, no light, no footpaths, just tarps and forts— and his mamá, standing there, clueless beside him, often got drunk and would end up naked on top of the old man. Ramón was just an outsider from La Isla. He was a tailor with an office in Bogotá. His house was too big. They would not have it.

So these two messengers of justice went straight to the school, their forces swelling with the idle, the unemployed, who bore kitchen knives, clubs, shovels, and, believing Ramón to be marooned within the office, pushed at the walls of that wooden box, trying to knock it off of its footings. They threw mud and rocks at the sides of all the buildings, and the children crawled beneath their desks. Soon their parents arrived to confront the mob, but hearing that Ramón had attempted to deprive their children of access to Encyclopedias Británicas, they joined the others in prying open the door.

He was gone. They snatched up bags of United Nations rice, yogurt, cookies, vegetable oil, and ran off in different directions. A mother swung the blade of a shovel through Ramón's computer screen and was tackled by another mother who believed computers to be divine and had intended to steal it. They dismantled his desk and stole his chair. They grabbed books, whiteboards, pencils, and a propane tank with a stove.

Violence was the one cure. All afternoon, under a hot mountain sun, while la Coca sold her calls and Hernán made up for lost sleep, the mob roamed in search of the tailor, calling at his two-story house, where Marta said through a closed door that she had not seen him for a month, and so back to Antonio's to interrogate him and retrieve what they thought was the complete set of encyclopedias. When they heard that Ramón had been spotted on la Gran Vía, they went back to the wooden school. They tore it to pieces, the doors unhinged, its tables carried off, the roofing undone piece by piece, while children of the afternoon session showed up in their blue sweaters to no teachers, no desks, their books rotting and bloated in the mud, as the mountain weather changed in a blink, and rain began to spoil what the mob had not.

By evening there was a strong movement to expel Ramón forever. By midnight another movement emerged to forgive him completely. They would hang the thieves. They would fix up the school. It was the future of their children.

CHAPTER TWENTY-NINE

At 6:00 A.M. the first bright-yellow bowl rolled up the assembly line to Station 8, and Alba grabbed it, scraping off a boil. The first ones had any number of flaws. She cleaned her blade on the side of her pants and watched for the next, working fast so she did not have to hit the red button and stall the line. Not easy work. Gloves would be nice, but precision at Station 8 was everything, and already her day seemed long, as she struggled to catch her breath before the steady passage of bowls and plates and pitchers. She raised up one foot to rest it. She poked at an itch in her crotch, wondered if she was bleeding. There were days she felt her dead babies inside her still, and she blamed the earwax for trapping the crazy idea in her head.

The line went faster as the temperature rose. Ahead, the rushing, careless bitches were the young ones who flirted with the managers, sucked them off in the closets by the cafeteria, and ascended fast to better stations like hers. No one wanted Station 1 at the vats of liquid plastic or 2, the molding zone. Station 8 was on the cooling side but not so lucky as 12, the loading dock, where the plastic got stacked, shrink-wrapped, and boxed, and, no goggles, you could sneak air through the half-open door. Alba would be there now if she had gone into the bathroom with the albino manager. Was it worth it?

The young ones said it was. It's your body, they said, it's your power. You're giving it away already.

The albino had fixed her time card once and bought her a lulo juice in the cafeteria. Later, he cornered her among the vats of Station 1 and she told him that she was contagious. In what way? he had asked.

"My God," Cintia said, her only friend here, rushing by from Station 7 with a nasty cut on her thumb. "What a way to start!"

"Are you OK?" Alba put her finger on the red button.

If Cintia were fired, Alba might not make it. Alone in the factory, the bitches would close in on her—too old, they'd say, and blame her for any mistake.

Modern fans hung from the ceiling but only spun for the inspectors who rarely came. The economy had slumped. The managers fretted upstairs in the air-conditioned offices, arriving late, leaving early, and, in between, gazing at computers and butts. Alba had guerrilla thoughts. Why not stick a screwdriver into the assembly line, pull some wires on the vats, hold a manager's head over liquid plastic to make him inhale the fumes. Walk out in the middle of a shift and catch a bus to anywhere.

A coughing noise erupted, and the line stalled. She lifted one foot off the floor and leaned on the warm conveyer belt to rest. The whole place went dark. She saw nothing but a pin of light from the loading dock. Women pulled off their bandanas to wipe their necks and eyes in the dark. No one dared try to leave with all the sharp edges on the line. They stood still, spitting out the bitter taste of cooked plastic, waiting for the flashlights of the managers to poke out from the glass doors of the second floor.

"Afuera!" the albino manager yelled, "Salimos, señoras, salimos."

The women filed out into the muddy lot, a fine mist blowing against their faces as they looked northward at the city to see if it was in flames or under siege by the guerrillas. Distant antennas were the only lit thing. An angry seagull squawked at them all. The nearby market, a section of Abastos, paused then resumed, the buses zooming by at their usual speed. No one had clocked out.

"Qué carajo," Cintia said, a thick bandage over her thumb, the deep red impress of her goggles around her eyes. She had already lost her pinky finger in a previous accident.

"I feel sick," Alba said, "even with this break. We'll see if they pay it. And your thumb?"

"You may not see me here tomorrow."

They lit cigarettes, and Alba counted the minutes, pleased at the darkness of the city. The factory seemed an ancient, aluminum ark, rusted, streaming with rain, beached on the banks of el río Bogotá.

"Señora, you," the albino manager called from the door of the factory. "I wanted to ask you something."

Alba felt the eyes of each woman pushing her forward. The albino had strange tastes.

Inside, the generator lit the offices but not the assembly area, so the plastic was hardening, certain pieces jammed in the molds, while others stood defective on the line.

Alba sat on a metal folding chair in the upstairs office, a bright room of three metal desks with computers and lots of cables snaking around them. A rose-scented air freshener was plugged into the wall, but the plastic fumes overpowered it. The albino looked clean of the world's grime, stripped of his skin, perhaps cleaner than she could ever get in Lidia's deep tub with the water that had to come from so far away. The women said the albino might jump across the desk and rub his face in your crotch. You had to kiss him, and then the easy way out was to get his pants off and give him head.

Milton had told her that he could kill anyone for her—anyone, which was his way of saying, I love you, mamá, but he never visited anymore. Only Hernán could have an office like this someday. She saw him hunched over a desk with the diagram of a factory, a list of human numbers, a graph of production. He would not force sex with the employees. He was a thief, the neighbors said, had helped ruin Ramón's school, but she knew better.

"Where are you from?" the albino said.

"Caucasia, but I stay in Soacha with my sister."

"Ah, Soacha. I have a friend there. It's nice, but not as nice as they think, no, but fine. It's cheap. Well, the reason I want to talk to you is that I am going to move you. We hardly waste a piece with you at Station 8. You are older. I think you could use the air, no? The pay is ten thousand pesos more per week. You will be the final check before our distributor. You have good eyes. You guard the integrity of the company."

"Thank you," she said.

"You girls," he said, standing up, and she braced herself. "You are the heartbeat of this business. I wish we could pay more." He picked up a pencil and drilled at his cheek with the eraser. "You can go."

She went to the door, holding up her hand to thank him, then hiding it in her frock. He made a squeaking noise. When she grabbed the door handle, he already had both hands hooked to her hip bones and was twisting her into a file cabinet, trying to jerk down her thick blue workpants. She helped him. She bent forward and spread her legs. He placed one hand on her back, but then he was just fucking himself. She knew the sound. A minute or so passed, and he squeaked again and rubbed the semen on her ass.

"Go," he said. "Por favor. Go outside."

She paused on the steps, waiting for her eyes to adjust to the dark of the factory and felt the cool gel running beneath her pants. Why hadn't the other girls told her? She began to laugh in the fashion of actresses in silent movies, wagging her head and gulping air. She stood outside, lit a cigarette while Cintia continued to stare at her bloody thumb held up against the mist. The women judged Alba's face and easy stance as guilty, but were more engaged by the prospect of going home early for the day.

"Y?" Cintia said. "And?"

"My God," Alba said, her laughter surging up into her tired pink eyes, her tongue. "He's a maricón. That's all."

CHAPTER THIRTY

THEIR HOUSE, BUILT in the very center of el Progreso, had once
failed as a cantina, and Hernán wondered if, dug solidly into the
earth or not, it might fail as a house, too. La Coca had tried to make
the bare room a warm place—plastic roses shoved into a jar of water,
a small portrait of a happy-looking Virgin in a bed sheet, flowery
fabric hung over the mold-stained brick of the kitchen wall, a love
poem taped above the bed—but some places never yield in beauty.

It was hard to be comfortable in April. Rather than clean, the rain
was dredging up all the shame of the neighborhood, the failed sewage pipes, dead dogs, and everything was covered in a sticky gray
film of mud. Wind slapped down on the neighboring roofs, on the
abandoned school, and some poor neighbor might call through the
door in a second, Hernán thought, asking for help with flooding.
For their own roof, la Coca had set extra rocks on the corners and
seams, and then went out to get ripped off by the butcher on chick-
en parts for a stew when she should have bought just eggs.

Something hot and different, she had said.

The door, its boards swelling with the water, slipped open, a puddle seeping through a rag at the threshold. The cell phone had gone
dead. La Coca dialed numbers and listened. Give us another month,
she said to it, but the phone was quiet. This triggered an argument
about who did more for the future of the baby, and it lasted all afternoon, first in quiet, hissing voices so the neighbors wouldn't hear,

and then with the rain they said everything they wanted and loudly. La Coca called him a thief, a dead thief, a weak lover, and the main reason she was not in school. He called her a rich girl. He told her to go home to Riki and get her cut, but what he was really saying was what they both felt—this might be all of it, that he might fail the government exam, that his capacity for greatness was like everyone else's: zero.

Hernán chewed a piece of rancid chicken from the stew, a coppery taste, no lime, no cilantro, and he spit the bones back into the bowl. He sat in a tiny chair at a red plastic children's table Lidia had taken from La Esperanza. At the counter, la Coca ladled soup into a bowl for herself, then dumped it back into the pot.

"It's fine," he had said. "We can borrow money from Alba."

To be safe—Hernán had been walking straight to school in the mornings, straight home to the cantina house in the afternoon, and did not spend time on the corners, the soccer court, the arcades, because everyone knew of his role in the robbery. Thus, he would serve—as Ramón's young nephew, hated by some for being tall, by others for being one of the four muchachos who studied across the lagoon with the pretty girls in their flannel skirts at the private and only good school in Cazucá—as the easy villain to punish for the downfall of what had been an all right school after all, notorious, and not just a little, for the glorious visit from the U.S. ambassador who looked out on the neighborhood and saw an opportunity to do good.

"It stinks in here," she said.

"It's the propane," he said. "I'll fix it."

"Are you sure the chicken's not bad?"

"It's fine."

But it was not fine. Both sensed that the excitement of the last eight months, sharing a bed, thinking of a new family together, had turned over so they wondered if they might be as typical as all the novios in all the back-alley shacks of Cazucá.

She brushed past him and stretched out across the bed, covering her face with her hands as if the yellow bulb strung across the roof were too much.

Just then, rain tested the house, tearing at the loose sheets of metal roofing. He felt hot blood in his ears, a shiver rising from his wet feet to his neck. He slurped salty broth from the spoon. It was early, not yet three o'clock in the afternoon, an hour when he still felt the pull of their needs, when he should find a way to hustle a few thousand pesos off the streets.

He grasped a chicken claw between his teeth, the jagged root of the ankle sharp on his tongue, and wagged his head.

"How is it?" la Coca said into the mattress, untying the pink bandana from her hair.

"It's delicious!"

"Why don't we turn on the television?" she asked. "Or you could read me something. Are you ready for your test? You haven't studied much."

She was close enough that with one lunge forward he could pin her down and poke her in the chest. Show her. She sat up and twisted the dial with pliers, and the television snapped into life, one channel spinning between color and static. Removing her slippers, she stood on the bed and reached up with the pink bandana to loosen the lightbulb. The television threw blue paint onto her pale face and hands—it froze her wide mouth, her good teeth.

"Don't lie to me," she said. "The stew is awful."

He dipped his spoon into the dark bowl and dug for a safe potato or carrot. "I could read you something."

"I'm tired of *T*," she said. "Read one of your textbooks."

"She's tired of *T*," he announced.

"When are you leaving?"

He stood up to press his fist against the water-heavy roof, raising it a little, as water splashed down the side. He stepped past her,

170

picked up a Bible from the nightstand and set it back down on a pile of rubber bands. "Two rooms would be better now that we have things. Maybe I could build one, a room for our kid. I could dig it into the slope."

"You need to get at least an eight hundred on the test," she said, "and get a scholarship and we'll borrow money and we'll move."

He reached for her.

"Get away!"

He looked at the television, the actors in fuzzy pajamas of static. A rock glanced off the roof, knocking water through a seam and onto the bed. They both listened.

"Son of a bitch," la Coca said. "Get under the bed. I'll answer."

Hernán snatched the canoe knife from the nightstand, folded it, and put it into his pocket. He peeked out the crack of the door, and Antonio stepped in with an encyclopedia in a garbage bag in one hand, a knapsack over his shoulder. He was wearing a drenched blue jean jacket. A giant bruise of blue and red layers bubbled up beneath his left eye and water dripped off his nose and lips, giving him a melting look.

"I brought you *H*," Antonio said, leaned down to kiss la Coca's cheek. "I thought with all the rain. How do you feel?"

"Sick," she said. "I should have bought eggs."

"You just need an antenna," Antonio said. "I'll make one."

"You got hit?" Hernán said.

"Don't be long," la Coca said, looking at Antonio. "I won't wait. They were talking about a new list at the store, about you both being on it, the whole gang. Everyone knows, and they said there's a mule stuck in the lagoon, paralyzed from drinking it."

"Whose mule?" Antonio said. "Ramón's?"

"Your eye," Hernán said. "You got popped. By who, parce?"

"There's always a list," Antonio said to la Coca. "No more footprints. Hah!" He looked at her in an odd, heavy way. "We'll be back soon. They know that I stole the encyclopedias. They know me. El Pollito is fine. He'll bring you something sweet."

"Sweet money," she said, "that's what I want."

Hernán stared at Antonio as if to access his thoughts and shape them into his own. Antonio looked back similarly.

"Who hit you?" Hernán said.

"I have a plan."

*

In Cazucá there were no flat roads, no smooth roads, no straight roads. In many houses, you sat at the table and watched your cup lean and slide down. You had sex at a natural incline. You were used to it. So Hernán tried to straighten his thoughts, to level out his plans so that they looked as clean and round and possible as eggs in the carton. It was an arduous task for a tall kid without a father, without more than three thousand pesos in his pocket at any time, knowing that his complete name, Hernán Vargas Rodríguez, appeared in killer handwriting on some local death list, or so they said, for these lists, according to gossip, were both literal and figurative. After dark, he would be stopped on the bridge over the drainage, and they would place his ID card next to the column of names on the back of an envelope. Or his name, his image floated in the mind of someone local, respected, a store owner who smiled at him and asked about his life as he made change, and then went out one night with the hoods, and they exterminated him, a necessary act to give the neighborhood a semblance of order, to scare off other thieves and educate the children.

Hernán knew that if he dwelled on all the curves and steep ups of his days, he would lose control. He would lose focus of his history book, the colonies, the imperialism, the slavery, the freedom, the capitalism. He would pick a fight with one of the few other male students and rub the kid's face in his own blood. He would show

172

the girls he was number one, which was a straight, even thing to be. Finally, he would go home and hold down pregnant la Coca, call her Carmen, and slap her face if she was rude to him. He would forget the straightest and simplest thing he ever did, which was dig for treasure, going by feel along the edges of the marsh and Cuturú landfill, looking for the most uninviting spots with coral snakes and shit, knowing, as he stomped the blade of the shovel into deeper soil, he might easily trip a landmine and become crippled or bleed to death. He read recently in his geography book that at fifteen feet below the surface of the earth the temperature was constant. Every morning he attempted to establish that temperature in his mind, but he found himself wavering in the days of the growing baby, from hot to cold to hot, at one moment despising la Coca, ready to skip town with Antonio who had a thousand cousins in safer places, like Honda, like barrio Santa Fé in Bogotá, where they could dedicate themselves completely to crime. At the other moment, which was now, he was hesitant to leave her at all. He asked Antonio to wait just beneath the limited eave of their roof.

"This could be something good," he said to her, and he promised to hurry, just down to San Mateo and back. He'd bring her something. What?

She sat cross-legged on the bed, flipping through the pages of *H*, pausing at certain photos or words. "I might commit suicide," she said, and then, "Chocolate."

"Fine."

He slammed the door shut and walked out into the rain, shaking his head while Antonio, hearing it all, imitated la Coca's voice in a lunatic soprano, "Chocolate, chocolate, chocolate." Foam was everywhere on the road. They walked around it, having to duck a sizable chunk wheeling toward them in front of the abandoned school.

"Where are we meeting him?" Hernán said.

"At the Olímpico in Unisur, in the vegetable section."

"Really?"

No, Antonio explained. They were going to the park, and Hernán was not supposed to talk.

Night was hours away but it seemed to be falling anyway, as buses came up the hill with their bright lights on, and Hernán pulled his hood over his head. On the edges of San Mateo, new three-story high-rises of government housing had been finished, tiny apartments with barred windows, high fences round them. They stopped to admire them and wondered how one got a deal like this. No graffiti marked the walls yet. The glass was new and shined under the rain. A couple little kids kicked a soccer ball at each other within the fence, and stopped to stare at Antonio.

"Vamos," Antonio said. "They know me."

They took a roundabout way, staying off the main road, to arrive at the park. Antonio's contact, his hope, sitting on the bench under a red umbrella, was Richard Galindo. He looked to Hernán like a soldier, his face stitched up and spilling off its sharp bones, his eyes worn inward from watching. Despite the cold turning his arms pink, he wore a lemon-pastel-striped shirt with a white collar. Pointing far off the margins of his face, his eyes widened every time Antonio said anything, no matter how ordinary. The first time Antonio had gone to him Richard had bought him coffee and empanadas to warm up. He had offered to move their encyclopedias, but his eyes widened and his tongue clicked when he learned that the set was not complete. "Get me a computer," he said now. "I can move that."

The park had one dying tree at the center, a giant circle of sand with only one slide, clogged up with a dozen kids struggling to squirm down in their wet clothes, and the rest was concrete with a basketball court, hoops with no nets, and all of it surrounded by yellow brick buildings that served as a canvas for the sweeping red and black graffiti, marred by misspellings, failed attempts at erasure, question marks, exclamation points, names of easy girls and beloved girls, hated boys, dead boys. In contrast to this, Hernán imagined the clean columns of questions from the government test, questions to stump a poor kid, a clock ticking loudly at the front of the room, a proctor staring at him alone in his desk in a row of desks where everyone bent forward and tried to breathe calmly yet hurry forward. If you panic, you fail, Cate had said, and she had not panicked. She was the bright star hanging above Ramón's house with her life in Bogotá.

Richard looked at Hernán and up at the sky, and his eyes widened. He scratched at his scars and sniffed compulsively through a red nose. He said he had something for them, for two friends, muchachos of their strength, of their skill set, but only maybe.

"What skills?" Antonio asked.

"Berracos. Risktakers. I know things about you," Richard said. "I've been studying the situation here, and I know who's who. Your friend is not important, but if you need him, he is included in the contract. No problem. He fits."

"What contract?" Antonio said.

"It's a maybe," Richard said, "but real money, a little unclean, but nothing dangerous. You would have to travel for a couple months. I can guarantee your safety. Come next week with your decision and I can confirm it."

"What's the work?" Hernán said.

"What?" Richard seemed baffled by the question.

"How can we decide if we don't know what it is?"

Richard looked away. "Not now. I can't be specific. Basically, you will be carrying something for us, you and some others. We give you the equipment, but then you carry it from one point to another, Town X to Town Z, not too far and not too dangerous. You do this twice, three times, and it's easy. We just need you to help us avoid some checkpoints. I'll tell you that I work for the military and that's why we can't do certain things the way you can. It's work. A hundred muchachos will grab it if you don't. No? We take a bus north to a place near Bucaramanga and that's how you get there. What else? The money is good."

CHAPTER THIRTY-ONE

DON RAFAEL HAD BEEN a history teacher in Barranquilla, his wife killed at the market while a gunman aimed for him, getting only the top of his left ear and a piece of scalp where hair no longer grew. Escaping any second attempts on his life, he had come to Bogotá and to Hernán's school, Los Pinos, as a teacher of language and writing. He was of old money on the coast, his father once the director of public relations for the governor, but that money was gone. He usually wore black shirts buttoned to the collar, priest-like, and perched on his white nose, thick as aquarium glass, spectacles that made him seem as if he were eyeing his way into the soft legs and blue flannel skirts of the girls, as he lusted distractedly for all the girls of Buenos Aires, the neighborhood that rose up a steep ravine on the far end of the lagoon and contained the school.

They read a severely abridged version of the *Odyssey,* with an illustration of Odysseus lashed to the mast of the ship and skinny tit-heavy sirens perched on precipices and singing. Don Rafael encouraged any parallels between the Argonauts, the never-ending Trojan War, and their own country's violent history. Twenty years ago, he said, the majority of Colombians lived in el campo, only a few in the cities. Now it was the opposite, the cities immense, which was fine by the capitalist model, as farmers were converted into hands of industry, but here the model had failed. And to reverse this trend? Forget it. The work was done.

"And el Presidente Uribe?" the class would ask, for they loved him, as did all the poor in those hills, imagining he was one of them, un macho, un duro, the one to win the war.

"You don't understand," Don Rafael said. "There *is* no war. Uribe is not of the fifteen ruling families, the Pastranas, the Gavirias, the Santos, the Londoños, the Turbays, the Betancourts. He is from Medellín, a hit man, a vulgarian. They brought him in to do the dirty work, and later they can blame all the atrocities on him. Their hands must be clean for the cocktail parties in Paris and London and New York. Watch. They have to get rid of him soon. To the people, to the poor around here, he's the messiah, but to them he is new money, un criminal."

"But he's winning," they said. "What about Iván Ríos, Raúl Reyes, Mono Joy Joy, and all the comandantes dead? The guerrilleros are losing."

He slapped the chalkboard for emphasis. He was sweating, and though his speech was even-keeled and soft, there were years of fury in it.

"The guerrilleros are fine, and they can hide forever," he continued. "They are only symptoms of the disease. You don't cure by killing symptoms. The roots just keep growing deeper into the soil until you look out your window and you say what the fuck are we going to do about all these poor people? Don't tell me it has always been this way."

Hernán nodded, wrote *roots too deep*.

"A fictitious war never ends," Don Rafael continued. "If it ends, there would be no excuse for half the population to eat their own shit. There would be a new guerrilla, or they would have to invent one. This one serves their purposes. They drink their tea with their pinkies in the air."

"Who? Who? Who?"

"The fifteen ruling families and all the other climbers and gringos and Europeans. The war is their project. They say look this way, it's out of control, and in a day their machinery has replaced your farm, your culture. Thus giving birth to the culture of death, and the earth, my friends, is full of your bones."

"And the rivers," Hernán chimed in.

"My God! Yes! The rivers! So go home and reproduce. Why not? Don't blame the killers. Don't blame Pablo Escobar! Blame the rich and their great paranoia. Who will cure them?"

Later, as Hernán and Marta were walking away from school and down the shore of the lagoon to the soccer court, she said, "Don Rafael is going to get killed if he keeps talking like that. Watch. They already call him a guerrillero."

"He hates the guerrilleros," Hernán said.

"Doesn't matter. People are simple."

"And if it's true what he says?"

"Look at what's true. Papá is stuck in his tailor shop in Bogotá because of you. Antonio could be face down on la Gran Vía, and my baby?"

"Why have babies at all?" he said. He leaned into her as a bus passed and covered them with dust. It had not rained in weeks, and their tongues were chalky.

"Because it's in me. It's in la Coca. Idiot."

They came over the lip of earth and down onto the sun-whitened soccer court, the sidelines worn away. No one had come to play. Here they gained a clear view of the road switching back uphill from Soacha. Idling at a station of contraband gas was a red pickup truck. He pointed at it. They hurried into the pines, out of sight, and if you happened to glance at the causeway that day, you would see a tall boy with a faint mustache, fast-walking, almost running, with two backpacks, the second belonging to a pregnant girl galloping behind him.

"What I don't understand," Hernán said when they were locked indoors, sweating from the climb, in Lidia's house, "is why Odysseus wouldn't just stay safe with his nymph Calypso. What does Penelope have?"

"If you don't know yet," Marta said, "then forget it."

"Do you still hate la Coca?"

"I love her now. We just needed a fight."

The image of the television switched in and out of focus to reveal the paramilitaries laying down their camouflage and rifles on a table. They looked like Nazis with their shaved heads, mean, sculpted faces, unhappy in their disarming. What awaited them in civilization was poverty, women who had to be seduced, not raped, food to be paid for in supermarkets, money earned a few pesos at a time. They had no skills.

"We'll be seeing them soon," he said and actually felt bad for the killers. "No chance for these pendejos."

"What about Milton?"

"True. He's OK for now."

"And you? Your test is soon."

He thought of home, of the papers with practice questions, stapled, folded, circled in red pencil, some of them very hard.

"One week," he said. "I should go study."

CHAPTER THIRTY-TWO

PAST GLOOMY ROTTWEILERS on short leashes and guards with twelve-gauge shotguns pointed into the redbrick steps, they climbed through the gateway of la Universidad Javeriana. The inner paths were muffled by the pine trees and varied buildings of blue reflective glass windows and steep-slanted roofs. On limestone benches or within the cafeterias, students sat with thick books, phones against their ears, saying they were in a hurry but not hurrying. Hernán had shaved the peach fuzz off his face, his long legs stiff and slow in new jeans. La Coca wore black slacks, a tight red polyester V-neck, her face redesigned with lipstick, eye shadow, rouge, as if for a fancy ball. Both had washed their hair. Both had scraped the mud from their shoes. Neither could say why they had traveled so far from home for a consultation at the pretty Jesuit university hospital, so far north into Bogotá, except to hear the baby's heart.

They followed the smell of toast and tobacco smoke into one of the cafeterias to buy coffee. They sat as if students. Each held one of the expanded, rain-damaged books from Ramón's dead school.

They took a number in the waiting area, filled out the registration papers, and waited in the hard blue plastic chairs. The floors had potted plants, and the blue walls were adorned with pastel pictures of palms and beaches, umbrellas and sandcastles. After an hour, a nurse called for "Carmen" and led la Coca alone through four heavy automatic doors to a tiny white room, handing her the pink gown and telling her to take off everything, to sit on the table with the metal stirrups.

Someone knocked. She said nothing. The door opened to a tall blond young man who introduced himself as a student in his fourth year of medicine. He shook her hand, pronounced her real name twice, and surprised her by suddenly grazing her belly with the back of his index finger. His face was an ivory carnival mask, a pointy nose and very deep nostrils. The face of a gomelo, a two-name rich boy, a Luis Carlos or Miguel Ángel, his white coat clean with the blue shield of the university. A white coat would be waiting for her too, someday, she dreamed, and, as a nurse or anything close to a doctor, she would be able to examine a poor girl like herself who would have paid the sixty thousand pesos and would expect some miracle from the building itself, expecting the coffee to taste rich and nutty in the cafeteria when it was actually burned.

The student examined her throat. "A bit red," he said, and asked her whether her quality of life had increased or decreased since the pregnancy.

"Increased," she said without thinking.

"Your mucus membranes are white, Carmen," he said, looking into her nostrils. "Do you have allergies?"

"No," she said. "No."

He looked and blew inside her ears. He stood beside her to listen to her heart, starting with the stethoscope on her left breast, sliding it across to the right, then onto her back, and she breathed dramatically, romantically, convinced she was doing it well. He touched the bandage on the back of her neck and asked about it.

"A fight," she said.

He was slow. She wanted him to say the exam was done and she was fine.

"I'll talk to the doctor," he said, "to tell him everything I know."

The student returned with the real doctor who wore filthy, gold-rimmed glasses. He made a number of dubious gestures, putting one hand on the wall, then reaching down to touch a burned spot on the linoleum floor before he washed his hands. He did something unexpected: he listened to her heart with his stethoscope, knowing it had been done, but he could not trust the student with his pointy nose, for he was truly concerned with the measurement of the beats. He said nothing. He did not try to teach or breathe on her like the student. She smelled the mint on his breath, the bleach in his white coat. His fingers were thick as a workman's.

"How is it?" she said.

"What?" the doctor said.

He looked through the murk of his glasses and into her eyes with sympathy.

"Your heart sounds fine," he said. "Breathe easy."

He checked her pulse from different angles, three spots on her neck, on her wrist, an artery just below her hip bones, and she shivered at that.

"Where do you live?" the doctor said.

"Cazucá."

"I don't know what that is."

He looked at his student while he put on blue latex gloves. Yes, this was why she was here. Under the bright lights. His eyes seemed uninterested in her open gown.

"I don't know what that is," he repeated, easing her knees open, clamping her calves within the metal stirrups. He bumped into the student who was trying to clamp down the other leg.

"Step back," he said. "Just watch."

"Excuse me," the student said.

"The city," the doctor said with one finger inside of her, "is growing too fast for me to know. The city is so strange for a man of my age who knew it as a town, quiet enough to hear cowbells at night. You didn't have to wear a face mask to walk on la Séptima."

"Cazucá is near Soacha," the student said, staring down inquisitively at her vagina.

"Yes," she said. "Near Soacha."

"Relax," the doctor said.

Her throat swelled. How embarrassing to have a difficult vagina in a cold room, but it was not so painful as he fit in more fingers, pushing on her pelvis with his other hand and inserting a tool.

"Cazucá," the doctor said. "It sounds like a song." He looked up at her. "Is it?"

She looked up at the fixtures of fluorescent light. His student watched over his shoulder, learning. Maybe it was a spasm of gas, maybe hunger. She burped, and her stomach growled. The doctor looked up.

"Excuse me," she said.

"You'll be eating more," the doctor said, "but get exercise too."

He told his student to put on gloves—no one asked her if she minded, if she had time—and told him what to check for, then watched, as the student felt her. She looked up hard at the ceiling. They recognize me in just the pink gown, she thought, in just my pubic hair, in my heartbeats, my voice. I am curious to them.

The room smelled now like a swimming pool, and her mouth was parched. She leaned her legs against the cold stirrups. She was pretty—that was why they delayed—even if her makeup was cheap. She could feel a fast pulse in her thighs, her face turning pink, but they did not look at her face. Her stomach growled again, an upheaval of gas.

The doctor pulled off his gloves and held out a soft hand to shake hers. He smiled. He took rapid breaths through his nose.

"Carmen of Cazucá," he said. "Good to know you, to learn something about the new city. I can refer you to a doctor in Soacha for the ultrasound. It must have taken you over an hour to get here. Did you come alone?"

"With my boyfriend," she said. "We thought this hospital was superior."

The student kept his gloves on. Please don't leave us, she wanted to say to the doctor, but did not want to embarrass the student. She draped the gown over her knees. She unclamped her legs from the stirrups, banging them on the sides of the table. Her heart was worth hearing now, a great traffic of blood.

"I want to change," she said. "Can I?"

"In three weeks," the doctor said, "you should get another exam. Let me go find the number my colleague in Soacha. Do you have any other questions?"

She had not asked any.

"Am I fine?" she asked weakly. "I came here for—I wanted to hear the baby's heart—"

"We don't have the equipment here for an ultrasound, not in this room. You have to make a separate appointment, but why come so far again?"

"Is it expensive?"

"It's necessary," he said, opening the door. "Eat well. You are underweight. Get a bandeja paisa."

"Thank you," she said, because it was over, she was healthy, her warm black slacks folded on the floor.

"Thanks for your patience with me," the student said, his stethoscope hanging over his neck, his hands still gloved.

"Go eat," the doctor said. "Eat well."

*

La Coca swallowed another acidic burp of hunger as she found Hernán hunched over the same foam cup of coffee in the cafeteria, a smear of mustard on his chin. The place was quiet now. Blue-frocked women were cleaning tables with bleach-soaked rags, and a few students slept on top of their books. No one noticed her, dressed up and of no interest.

"They listened to my heart a lot," she said.

"Why would they do that?"

"Can we walk around a little? I don't think anyone knows if we are students or not."

"Fine."

Just to see the artificial green turf running track and soccer field, the broad blue-glass wall of the gymnasium in a stand of eucalyptus trees, a group of boys chasing after an airborne white Frisbee and yelling directions at one another, in some game she had never seen. Huddles of smokers and talkers and sprawled-out readers in the grass; boyfriends with their heads in the laps of girlfriends. Lethargy reigned over the whole campus. Their voices rose and fell rhythmically, confidently. A black man with yellow eyes pushed a wheelbarrow stacked high with sod folded up like pastry dough. The radios of the security guards cackled with messages and static that made her uneasy.

They sat down on a bench where sharp sun shone directly through the old pine trees into their faces. It was an unaffordable place. Not for injustice or fate but because her father Riki was again crossing the country in his truck, a pussy-hound, a butt-hound, a wastrel, while Hernán's father was gone forever.

"Vamos," Hernán said. "What's the point?"

A girl lighting a cigarette seemed to hear. She looked above their heads, she laughed very carefully, as if for food in her mouth. No, not at them, about something else, something hilarious, and la Coca wanted to know what. Why was it so quiet? The screaming city was incarcerated behind the trees, permitting the practice of this religion of concentration and easy breathing. How nice to smell the eucalyptus and there returned the black man with his empty wheelbarrow and dreadful yellow eyes.

"The doctor said I should eat for two," la Coca said.

"At home we can make eggs. We can pick up meat."

186

"More eggs? Really?"

She wanted to talk to this smoking girl just to confirm she had a functioning voice, to ask where a certain classroom was, a bathroom, an exit, pretend as if she knew her from somewhere.

"Lots of money," Hernán sighed. "Lots."

"Maybe if you do well on the test."

"Not here."

"But it's Jesuit. I'm sure they have a scholarship."

"We'll see."

They stepped quickly down the redbrick stairs and onto the piss-stained sidewalk of la Séptima, into the diesel exhaust and bad breath and pizzas cooking and crowded wet garbage stink. They walked slowly south toward el centro. No security guards now. The air was rancid. Sellers stood everywhere frying things in the sun.

"It's a mistake," Hernán said, thinking of the money Alba had lent them to come here, "if all they did was listen to your heart. A waste."

"It's good to know. Otherwise you imagine it all day without any real images of what you want. I'd like to cure people."

"It's not like they paint it, not at all."

"Who?"

"The rich."

"I want to go home."

"There were some medical books in La Idea," he said. "They're around, in someone's hands, and I could find them."

Fine. They said he was the smartest in the school, so he would study and listen to her heart. He could tear the Frisbee down from the sky into the soft green turf where others reached and fell with the momentum of their sprinting. He could look up and blow a kiss at her with a biology book in her lap. She would be in such a hurry like the students.

*

187

On their way across the causeway into el Progreso, trying to decide what cut of meat they could afford, they were intercepted by Antonio in his sunglasses. He pushed them along the shore and up a back alley in the direction of Lidia's house.

"Bad rumors," Antonio said. "They're looking for us. Someone knocked on your door an hour ago. I thought you were dead."

Marta let them inside and kissed la Coca's cheek as if she had never bitten her. "Stay here as many nights as you want. Papá is still hiding at the tailor shop."

The neighbors grumbled about Antonio's presence; he put their children at risk, they told Lidia, their walls not nearly as thick as hers. She grumbled too, resigned to the mistakes of the young. Antonio slept with Marta who was about to give birth, and he vowed to be a real father, while Hernán and la Coca shared Caterín's old bed. They had fun, joking excitedly into the night, their lives at risk, so much that Alba had to shove toilet paper into her ears to sleep. Somehow, that same day, by buying or stealing them from the neighbors, still the leader of his gang, Antonio had recovered all but a few of the encyclopedias, which he then bagged up and buried one by one in the pines by the soccer court. He had even drawn up a map to remember where each was. He was waiting for word from Richard Galindo about this too-good-to-be-true job in the north, asking around in other neighborhoods to see what people knew about it.

The way to leave home was to not say good-bye, Antonio told Hernán the next morning when the girls had left to pick up clothes for la Coca. Antonio had no one but Marta who was bitter with his baby almost ready to be born, and he knew better than to explain a job like this. He advised Hernán to leave some money and a note on la Coca's pillow, at least, so she wouldn't think he left for nothing or that he was going by force. They would return with real money and in glory. They'd pay off a few of the community leaders, and buy a round at the cantina.

"You two are crazy," la Coca said, when Hernán told her later that night. They sat smoking on the roof, their backs against the stairway of the unfinished third story of Ramón's house. Downstairs, Antonio and Marta were having a similar fight, while Alba sat brainless in front of the television, as if watching a show about plastic, her day off wasted again in el centro with no sign of Wilfredo. That morning, a tall kid had turned up dead in the doorway of La Esperanza.

"I am going to save your life," la Coca said. "It's not only yours, and your test is in three days. What are you going to do? Take it and leave town?"

"I could call Olivia. She'd help us."

"You should have told me it was Richard Galindo. I danced with him one night when he was buying me beers in the cantina. He rubbed his hard-on all over my leg, but I was drunk so I didn't care. I couldn't see where I was stepping. So next thing I know I am in his lap and he's pouring rum into my mouth. I'm all alone and drunk, and then Antonio walks in and I'm saved. What's wrong with Antonio now? The same thing that is wrong with Riki, Ramón, and all of you. He thinks he's God. They are going to kill him. Not you. You are with me."

"Olivia told me she'd let me stay for a night or two. If not, I could probably go to the tailor shop."

"But why, if you are safe here?"

"People know where I am."

"Don't lie. But call her. Tell her it's Richard Galindo, and she'll know who he is. If you go, they'll make you a slave in the emerald mines or run drugs through Panamá. Who knows? Maybe you'd have to become a paramilitary. These are not real jobs, mi amor."

"Antonio's going."

"Not you."

CHAPTER THIRTY-THREE

WHETHER LIDIA WAS SORE from too much fucking the night before or sick with indigestion or hungry or just depressed, she would feel jabs of impossible longing on nights like these. She found herself alone in her bed, and wondered if she simply had more feelings than most people. I am alive, she thought, despite two births and so many beatings. I am not a piece of burlap to wipe your feet on.

She licked the coarse hem of sheet and lifted the wool blankets to smell her gas, her stomach turning with bad tomatoes and beef. She heard the first-floor door shut and wondered who had snuck inside or off into the night.

The room was cluttered with old clothes and broken chairs. A new poster of the ocean was peeling down, and if she had known that Ramón would be absent so long, she never would have asked for a second story. She would be happier in the crowded, warmer single room downstairs. If they had only filled the house with better stuff, with real framed pictures, with books, with a thick carpet for their cold feet, then Ramón would be here now and she could wake him, like in the first years when he was tireless and loved her smell, calling it a mix of banana tree and tropical rain. But he liked new smells, sniffing and sniffing wherever he was near a girl, on the street, in the store, on the bus.

Two weeks had passed since the robbery of La Idea. Lidia had not been home the day the mob came knocking, but the second she stepped foot in the neighborhood the gossip was upon her that Ramón was dead. She would have her public tantrum—who would not seize that opportunity?—but would never go like Alba to el centro and imagine him in the windows of high buildings. She would be a symbol of practicality—sell the house and move to Bosa, to Ciudad Bolívar, a place with pavement and pipes and better people. She would make up a new story for herself, no matter how tiring it seemed.

But Ramón, her little bug, her enano, was alive and working as usual, as he should have stayed, with needle and thread, but had not withdrawn his name from the ballot for city council in Soacha.

Mañana, Ramón had said on the phone that day, I'll come by and we'll go hang the banner with my picture on it. I'll make the promise of the pavement, the aqueduct, and I'll have my people around me. There are supporters still. Muchos.

No, she had said. Wait. Just be a tailor and let's sell the house.

She felt pressure in her abdomen. She dressed fast and went downstairs to the cold bathroom, sat on the toilet looking into the black tub, imagining it new again. Her knees ached from her squatting. I am old and gassy. Where did it begin?

When she stepped out to hurry back to her still-warm blankets, she found Marta at the table smoking Alba's cigarettes and realized it was dawn already.

"You'll hurt the baby," Lidia said. "Why?"

"I'm low," she said, covering up a piece of paper and folding it.

"Jam a knife into your heart. How romantic. What do you have?"

"A letter."

Lidia reached into the refrigerator and ate a piece of salty cheese, picked out a piece of papaya, so overripe she squeezed it against the roof of her mouth, turning it to juice. "Is your letter good?"

"I had never written one."

191

"Come upstairs, mi amor. It's too cold up there alone."

She waited, put her hand into Marta's thick hair and sniffed it. It smelled like old leather shoes, but she liked it. Maybe water would come tomorrow. They would all bathe in turn. They would all improve.

"Will there be water tomorrow?" Lidia said.

"I don't care."

"I'm going to get us another tank somehow. With everyone staying here now, it's good. I like this house crowded. Are you friends with la Coca again?"

"I just want people to respect me."

"Come upstairs. I need your heat. I've given away all my blankets."

"I want to be alone," Marta said.

"Now you do. Just wait. Soon you'll have your baby to worry about and I'll be dead. You'll have regrets you cannot imagine. Who left?"

"The muchachos went to Abastos to throw crates."

"It's already time? Of course it is. I feel safer when they're gone. I'm freezing. Come on."

The blankets had gone cold. Alone, she longed for humidity and the smell of plants, a hammock with a man or anything with warm blood, a dog, a cat, a new child. She wept. She thought about Caterín in some lecture pit in la Universidad Nacional, clicking her pierced tongue and thinking new ideas. Cate carried a layer of rich flesh on all her limbs, her voice tending to stall as her thoughts caught up, sharp thoughts, as she listened hard to every word you said now, and then stabbed you with this new way of thinking, using words not unlike those of the vests. It was impressive in the moment, but then Lidia forgot the words or what she had gotten from them. One Sunday, Cate brought over her boyfriend, un gomelo with a red-freckled face and very bad posture. He took a thorough tour of the house, an inventory tour, it seemed, and then thanked God for the generous food and asked for peace on earth. Lidia had laughed rudely in his face, Marta catching the laughing bug too, and it was too funny to ask for such things and not laugh, even if it made Caterín hate them.

"Marta!" Lidia yelled, loud enough to wake Alba before her alarm clock. "Por favor!" Cate was the one she loved the most, the one gone off to not lose hope, to pass this repetition of cold nights in better company.

CHAPTER THIRTY-FOUR

RAIN SOAKED THROUGH the cotton of their hoods and the thin nylon of their cheap windbreakers. Buses and taxis jammed the road. Passengers, dry with their eyes half-open, looked out the windows at a fractured city. The capital was flooding for real. Downhill came rippling streams over brick streets, and all around the sewers were expanding into garbage ponds. The wind tore at the broken umbrella Antonio had stolen from a man ordering coffee in a café. They tried to share it but ended up bumping into each other, switching it every other block, while the other got drenched. They passed a number of fancy bars where the rich youth drank beer and whiskey, dancing under colored lights, and each woman's beauty was enhanced threefold by good hygiene, an elaborate hairstyle, and clothing that fit perfectly around the curves of her body. At la avenida de Chile, they stopped to look up at the skyscrapers of Bogotá's Wall Street, Citibank, Microsoft, Bancolombia, and then turned up a steep slope into the first-world elegance of Rosales.

"Your name, señor?" the doorman said, eyeing the puddles they were making on the marble floor of the lobby.

"Buenas noches. I am Hernán, and he is Napoleón Bonaparte."

"A moment, please." He picked up a phone and pressed a button. "Buenas Noches, señora. Here are Hernán and Señor Bonaparte." He hung up. "She's coming down."

Next to a green sofa made of hard canvas cushions and white-washed bamboo, they leaned against the heat vents, which brought tears to their eyes. In the mirror, they seemed like uninspired terrorists from the mountains. Antonio put on his sunglasses and opened a bag of corn chips he had bought with the last of the money, crunching spectacularly in the silence and covering his face with powdered cheese. The doorman bowed his head into his chest and seemed to be asleep.

In Hernán's hand was a box of Chilean wine they had chosen from a row of boxes and dusty bottles in a corner store. It had been the gaudiest-looking one with golden vines, a virginesque figure with grapes in her hair, a fountain of red flowing into a bathtub beside her.

"It's wet out there," Hernán said to the doorman who did not look up.

The elevator beeped, and Olivia stepped out in a black Puma jogging suit. She looked sharp. She smelled like menthol cigarettes, and her wire-rim glasses gleamed green in the florescent light.

"Hola, chicos," she said, offering her smooth white cheek to Hernán, hitting him with her sharp chin, as if she did not want him to kiss her. She looked at the doorman whose head had slumped forward again.

"You came on an unfortunate night," she said, checking her watch. "My team is coming in a half-hour for a meeting, and I may have another guest from Tunja staying the night. What's wrong?"

Any night is fine, she had said. Just come. Don't even call.

"I'm going to go smoke," Antonio mumbled. The doorman buzzed the lock on the heavy glass door, and Antonio stepped out onto the brick steps where two men in black suits leaned against the bumper of a diplomat's SUV. The rain had stopped. Imprints of powdered cheese shined on the brass handle of the door.

"I don't trust him," Olivia said. They sat down on the green sofa. "You can stay, but all I know about him is he stabbed Doña Rita's son and has impregnated two girls from my theater workshop in La Isla."

"He's good people."

"Am I wrong about those girls?"

Hernán looked at the box of wine and wondered if in Italy the people actually bathed in it.

"I don't know him," she said. "I just know his look. I'm sorry."

"We should have called. That's what la Coca said."

"How is she? When is your test? Saturday, no?"

"We brought you this wine."

"I can help pay for the doctor's visit."

She did not take the wine from his hand, so it was not good. It was too cheap for her. He turned to the door, and the doorman pressed the buzzer. He gripped the brass handle, and the glass door felt stuck, like if he got it open now he might never open it again.

"But you can stay," she said. "No problem."

She came close and grabbed the handle. Her breath smelled like salad. Her eyes were watery and made him think of Alba. The green couch had been warm, and he could feel the cold sneaking through the crack in the door.

"Another time," he said. "Don't worry."

She jabbed out again with her white chin, and he kissed her full on the cheek, though he could have denied her that end—that all is good, we'll sleep on the street—but his response was polite and automatic.

"Here!" She shoved a folded ten-thousand-peso bill into his palm. "But stay. Just you."

"Let me talk to him," he said, touching the shoulder of her silky jogging suit. "Wait."

He walked out the buzzing door to find Antonio against the side of the building, the sunglasses on.

"Mierda," Hernán said. "I tried. She says you are too ugly and too fertile."

"Sure," Antonio said. "But fuck it."

"You could go to your uncle's in Santa Fé." He knew it was wrong—his desire to see her apartment. To see, that's all, what was above the city and behind Olivia and her vest.

"Let's drink the wine first."

Behind them the doorman sprayed the door handle and wiped it with a rag. Olivia put one hand against the front desk and pulled her foot up flat against her butt to stretch her quadriceps.

"You should try for her bed, parce," Antonio said.

"And you?"

"I told Richard I'm going. We leave from la avenida 19 with Carrera 30 at noon. If I see you, fine. If not, fine too. I'll be back in a couple months with some money. Tell Marta she's the only one."

"Call her."

"True. I should."

They hugged with force, Antonio so short that his head butted against Hernán's chest. Hernán watched him descend the slope into the gutters of the city, la Séptima a long line of frustrated brake lights. A doorman from another building stepped outside to watch him get off the block. That was life in northern Bogotá. No paramilitaries would find him here. Under a streetlamp, Antonio stopped to knife open the box of wine and took a long drink.

Olivia's walls were decorated by framed black-and-white photographs of indigenous people, their huts, and makeshift footbridges over Colombian rivers. Hernán checked each one in search of el río Puerco and felt a finger pressing sharply into the back of his neck, as he found familiar sights, the same beer signs onshore, the little buoys marking the rocks. But she didn't need decorations with such large windows, possessing her view of the growing metropolis, the slum, the suburbs, the airplanes landing in El Dorado. He wondered what it was like when the guerrillas blacked out the city. He'd like to see that from right here.

She ordered him to take what was—he realized, naked, unsure whether she was going to barge in—the first hot shower of his life. He stood under the sharp stream of water and expected it to go freezing cold. He sat down cross-legged and let it hit him. He had never been this clean, a better pleasure than any he'd ever known. Next to the sink was a clothes hamper, and he sorted through the contents, a pair of soiled mango-colored panties, too sexy for a woman like her. He found a razor in the shower and shaved off the little hairs of his mustache.

"You are a good person," he said to her at the table, eating a toasted ham-and-cheese sandwich, surprising himself.

"How long have I known you?" She didn't smile, for she had helped a lot of people and how much good had it done?

They talked about the early days in Cazucá, how not much improved, except that the green hills on the other side of the lagoon were covered with a million more shanties and there was running water in a few neighborhoods. Wilfredo might show up someday, she said. It happened.

"Do me a favor," Olivia said. There was nothing sexual at all in the way she reached out and touched his hands, and he realized that he had never really looked much at her face, nor had he seen her without a vest on. She still had the same small breasts, the somewhat muscular and broad shoulders of a man. Her face asked for a vacation. It had a veiny paleness, and tiny creases shot out from the sides of her eyes. Her nose was large, pointed, unlike the noses of Cazucá. "Have just one baby, Hernáncito. There are too many pregnant girls.

I feel defeated when I think about it. We can help you with one, but there are so many. I think you are going to do well on this test. I really do."

"If I don't?"

"I'll tutor you. You'll take it again."

There seemed to be an extra room, but she made him a bed on a white couch with a bloody wine stain on one arm, where his body was too long, the pillow too high for his head. With the lights off, the city floated there, bad things happening within the black space of the lights, shimmering a little, the planes still landing. The moan of a tenor saxophone played within the closed door of Olivia's room, and he could hear her humming along to it. She had stacks of heavy psychology and philosophy books on the coffee table, a notebook with quotes and page numbers and her ideas in red ink. When the light beneath her door went dark, he tiptoed around the kitchen, tasted her milk, and ate a green olive for the first time in his life, almost breaking a tooth on the pit. One cupboard was locked. There was a gray pork chop in the refrigerator, wasted, a large bouquet of broccoli gone brown, a jar of capers, another of pickled onions. He tried everything. The light beneath her bedroom door came on.

"Hernán?"

"I'm getting some water."

He rinsed his mouth out, crouched on the floor, and smiled at himself. The enthusiastic saxophone played again in her room. He heard the click of the lock on her door. Yes, he might creep through the dark, misunderstanding, as Antonio would, his place in the world, thinking they could load the bathtub with bubbles and use all of the lotions above the bathroom sink. You are safe from me, he wanted to tell her. He pressed his face into the cushions of the couch and knew he would never sleep and that she would not believe him.

CHAPTER THIRTY-FIVE

FROM A HILLSIDE ACROSS the highway one might observe the elegant main greenhouses of fine clear glass compared to others propped up into makeshift tents of blurry plastic, cheap enough to blow away in a storm but good enough for now to help satisfy the world's demand for flowers. Despite how dirty the work was, the grounds were fairly clean. Mangy cows grazed between the main structures and a leashed-up German shepherd guarded the entrance. What was once a farmhouse had been expanded piece by piece into a command center where clipboard-carrying managers directed the containers into the constant arrival of trucks. Like any work, it was a question of rhythm, a picker's efficiency easily checked by the number of containers he pushed to the door. The men who picked were not beautiful. They shined with stinky sweat, they swore at the pretty flowers, the malfunctioning sprinklers that soaked them, and imagined themselves trapped in some gardener's awful dream. Those who were not short walked permanently hunched over. They wore gloves, their hands raw, and carried clippers, stem-crusted steak knives, and rubber bands.

Wilfredo raced against this artificial summer, snipping at the opening roses. They would be sorted and hurried twenty miles to El Dorado International Airport and purchased in the capitals of the world. He imagined pale women in red underwear taking the trimmed stems into their lips and arching their backs for the ecstasy of Valentine's Day. At his back, Calipari, too old for the work, bent over with slow hands for the opened and ruined roses —flores nacionales, they called them—to be sold cheap on the street corners of Bogotá.

Wilfredo drank from a hose used to mist the flower beds of Greenhouse 87 and wiped a film of chemical sweat off his face. His body was shaped like a thick root, his mouth, peppered with bits of soil, shrunk into an unwanted smile. He would drop dead into velvety red petals, he thought, right here in the frenzy. He could think about a few things to distract himself from the endless boredom of picking: those pale women in red underwear with roses in their lips or his past life, contained in a protective ceramic jar so fragile that if he flicked it with his thumb, if he looked too closely, the whole thing broke and he had shit on his lap.

"I'll take these to the sorters," Calipari said, happy at their pace, speaking just to hear his voice, for there was no reason to explain the destination of a full bin.

Picking flowers was ruining Wilfredo's eyes. He went by feel, squeezing the crowns of the roses a little to know. Too often, he mixed opening flowers among the pristine blossoms, making the sorters curse Greenhouse 87 or wherever he was found. When they all failed, a bad flower flew north to the disliking eye of a florist, all the middlemen suffering a loss, which began with Wilfredo who would be demoted to the hellish carnations or find himself back on the street.

Having pushed out four containers in a just over an hour, done for now in Greenhouse 87 and getting a brief taste of outside air, Wilfredo and Calipari walked to Greenhouse 89, where one of the workers had passed out from exhaustion. They threw him into a bin of ugly, unsellable roses and pushed him out into the sun, joking that they might sneak him into a refrigerated truck and see if he made it to one of the capitals of the world.

It was pleasant to think about capitals of the world, with clean streets, sidewalk cafés, fireplaces, skating rinks, to travel with the flowers, but mostly, Wilfredo went backward. He saw himself lost in Bogotá, dirty and embarrassed, walking to Ramón's house the morning after his first day in Abastos. Did you forget me? he would say to Alba and Hernán someday soon on a visit, inviting them to a coffee and some sweet bread at the bakery, just to sit for a moment and look at each other. He would not speak in this vision. Only Hernán, an archeologist or detective, would speak of his travels to unearth artifacts and bodies and soil samples. Alba would hold his hand and recall their early days together, taking his boat to different quiet places on el río Puerco to fish. And Milton who had disappeared from Tuts's shop?

"Vamos, Wilfredo," Calipari said, biting an ugly rose off its stem and spitting it onto the ground. "It's time."

They boarded the green workers bus, which brought them downhill, merged onto the busy Panamerican Highway, and left them at the desolate plaza de Simón Bolívar. Employed in every direction, all the people had found temporary work at the greenhouses. The cathedral was closed. A woman squatted with pink knees on a blanket, selling papayas and DVDs and nail clippers, her head sideways to hear two teenage policemen sharing a cigarette against the cracked wall of a building damaged in the last earthquake. Through his bad eyes Wilfredo saw everything half-standing, as if there were always an earthquake, and the woman could easily have been his wife Alba and he wouldn't know it until he was upon her. He tried to say to Calipari that the policemen looked a lot like the ones who had robbed them, but his throat locked up in a yawn.

Down an alley from the main plaza, they climbed around a young woman sloshing the steps of their boarding house with a heavy gray mop. The woman gave Wilfredo a funny glance like she knew about something more than just the surface of his life.

"Done already?" she said. "How many?"

"Millions," Wilfredo said. "Two more days of roses."

"The exterminator came this morning. You'll smell it."

The boarding house had been a brothel until just a year ago when the mayor had ordered all sex business to the edge of the town in hopes of promoting tourism in the plaza. It was a spoiled and sagging building of soft cement walls and wood floors gouged by the sharp high heels of the whores. No matter the bleach, the incense, the scouring pads and good intentions of the cleaning lady, it reeked of sex and sweat, which, compared to some of the other places they had stayed, was not such a bad smell.

Their room was tiny, set in the back corner of the building, without windows but containing two comfortable beds set up on sharp iron frames. A bathroom with hot showers was down the hall, but both men fell headfirst onto their pillows, shoes on, and slept hard, even if the exterminator's poison had been too weak.

In four hours, the dependable clock in Wilfredo's head sounded its alarm, and he reached out with his eyes closed and shook Calipari.

"Vamos, hermano," Wilfredo said.

A year ago they had slowed for what they thought was a military barricade near Medellín. They decided to kill time in a café, the tables packed, forcing them to sit out of view of the truck. When they emerged, it was gone. Calipari ran one direction up the road, grabbing the first soldier he saw and telling him to radio ahead. They visited the paramilitary who ran the town, a fat kid in an open canvas shirt, sitting on the tailgate of an SUV. The kid listened with a grave smile and said no one stole on his territory, impossible. He offered Calipari a piece of gum. They tried to pay him to make calls, but he wouldn't take it, and they went back to wait at the café. Calipari checked the parking lot every so often to know if he was crazy, finding nothing but oil stains in the pavement. After a week, he knew his truck had been broken into a hundred parts for sale on the streets of Medellín.

When Calipari did not wake up, Wilfredo flipped on the lights.

The sheet was darkened by a line of urine stretching from his waist to his head. Wilfredo touched the veins on the sides of his neck and felt no pulse. He sat back down on his own bed and listened for breathing. A flea jumped. He would have to go finish his shift. Valentine's Day was close, this the last time to make money before they were laid off. He reached into Calipari's wet front pocket and found a tiny roll of bills, wiped them dry on the sheets, pulled off his shoe, and was about to put the cash below the insoles, when Calipari snatched it from his hands.

"I pissed on myself," Calipari said. "Mierda. I'm old."

"I thought you were dead, hermano."

"Not even close. I dreamed I was a rose. It was terrible."

The roses flew safely north, selling well, and everyone got paid on time, plus a sizable bonus. Facatativá entered a state of unofficial fiesta. A thousand people were trying to pry the new money away from the pickers. Calipari wanted to go straight to the whorehouse, even as Wilfredo explained that he was considering, as he did every payday, a visit to Alba.

"Not yet," Calipari argued, jerking his elbow above his head with a little plastic cup of rum in his fingers. "We need to burn a little money." His long legs branched out across the bed, his toenails clipped and feet oily with some miracle potion. He wore a new green leather jacket, and his hair was slicked back with gel.

Outside, taxis and buses jammed the borders of the central plaza. Vendors waved lottery tickets, discount cards for the brothels, fruit, fried coconut, and at the very center a white-faced mime, encircled by children, imitated whoever crossed his way. Yesterday, the mime had approached Wilfredo with his eyes squinted and his fists at his sides in the overdone posture of an ape. He turned when Wilfredo turned, making a shouting face, delighting the crowd, when Wilfredo screamed at him to back off.

"Let's go out the backdoor," Wilfredo said, putting the money he was willing to spend in his right pocket, the rest into a pouch sewn into the crotch of his underwear. "I want to avoid the mime."

They walked the main street, eyeing the shop windows for deals on jeans, boots, and shirts. Wilfredo stopped to ask about a yellow cotton dress Alba's size, touched the cash in his crotch, and said he'd be back. They ate roasted corn and fried beef pastries and drank beer among other pickers who were walking slowly in the same direction. As the dusk sky faded to black, they passed from the well-lit commercial blocks to a drab row of similar brick buildings, and up a long stairway to a bar with neon-pink lights, music so loud it did damage to the ears, and an assortment of barely clothed girls on stools, bored to death before the rush of men.

Wilfredo danced with a stiff-smiling girl about his height. She was chubby with no tits, a fairly large ass, and a wide-nosed freckled face he had come to recognize as one from rural Boyacá. The cheap bleach she had used to blonde her hair could not conceal the dark roots, the thickness of it. Her grandparents had probably raised potatoes and her parents were pickers of flowers, and, as Calipari said, Wilfredo never failed to choose the ugliest girl.

She led him to a tiny room with a single bulb hanging over a bed, pushed up against a shelf of glittery pink clothing. Her stiff smile disappeared. She undressed. Her skin was fuzzy with little hairs that pricked up from the cold, and she crouched wide like an animal on the bed.

"What's your name?" he said, touching the bone of her waist. "I'm Wilfredo."

"Regina," she garbled, as if her tongue were too much tired flesh. "It's ten thousand extra if you want me to do anything or to moan."

No, he did not need an active girl, a mime, he wanted things to be as they were. He took off just his jeans and underwear, keeping his socks on, and climbed onto her back. Moles along her spine formed a river if he connected them, curving up over her shoulder, and at one point he turned her over to see what happened to it, but then he had trouble. She was impatient. A warning knock shook the door. How long? He turned her over again and rushed, smacking his head sharply against the shelf above the bed. While he caught his breath and touched the deep cut on his forehead, she laughed in brusque inhalations, saying "Pobre, dios mío," handing him the corner of the sheet to soak up the blood. She laid him down and hopped up and down on him with a serious look on her face. Her technique worked. Like setting an anchor or pounding a nail clean into a board, his pleasure was modest. He was the mime, doing what men did beyond all the thin walls, cursing at the pressure of their orgasms.

She removed herself, and in a flash she was fully dressed, waiting for a tip. He gave her only a five thousand peso bill, but she pocketed it, thanked him, said, "Come back."

Did you forget me? he would say to Alba as soon as tomorrow, inviting her to a coffee and some sweet bread at the bakery, just to sit for a moment and look at each other. They had never been talkers. He would reach across the table for her stubby fingers, and whether she had a new boyfriend or not, she would hold his hand. There would be no mosquitoes, no river or any water nearby, no loud love songs from the cantina, and so it would not be like the first, happy section of their lives. It would be the afterlife, the postdisplacement, a respite in the rush to keep moving until one died. Would he stay? He might. He'd accept much less than the dreamed of hotel and blue-water pool on the coast—just a stinky storefront outside of Bogotá, a long glass cooler filled with chicken carcasses, fresh beef, baskets of eggs, butter, salty cheese, a bell on the door.

He dressed quickly and soon found himself at a table with Cali-pari at a different whorehouse, with better, younger girls, supposedly, but he wanted none of them. He paid for overpriced beers and drank himself into a safe remove from the colored light, the men—pickers, managers, truck drivers—who nodded at him, Greenhouse 87, as they walked around eyeing the women who glowed in his half-blind eyes like jellyfish.

"We might still get to that hotel with a pool," Calipari said, hunched sideways with his troublesome height. They seemed bound together by bad luck and the truth that they were bound to nothing else. "There are angles, hermano, that we don't see. Sex is one. You don't realize the aberrations of the people. We bring in the grotesques, the transvestites, a mule, the biggest meanest black women, and there we have our angle. See? We open a humble establishment, but from there who knows?"

"Who knows?" Wilfredo said and wondered if Calipari had been keeping him away from his wife. "There are new angles, but I'm old. I'm almost blind, hermano. What would my role be?"

Wilfredo wandered the dark streets alone. He lost his way for a while and didn't care. The stores were blocked with steel bars. A few pigeons sorted through the trash in the corners of the plaza. He entered a brightly lit call center—so drunk the acne-scarred youth stared at him with uncertainty—and sat down in a glass booth to call Alba or his brother Tuts or anyone who had known him when he was still a boatman, dialing once and failing, then resting his head on his arm for a nap.

He awoke briefly to see a streetlight oscillating above him, and felt his head bouncing on the curb, caught in the sewer gratings, as he was dragged by his ankles and thrown by busy hands into the back of a pickup truck. If it was the police, fine, but if not, he hoped they would kill him.

As they left the city, a spare tire rubbed against the side of his head and old rotten water sloshed beneath him. Just beyond the glow of an arc light, the truck stopped, and he felt the busy hands on his ankles again. He was launched onto the dirt and rolled over. "Kill me," he said, even though he had changed his mind about that.

They laughed, put their pistols to his balls, and he heard in their cracking voices that they were teenage policemen, this a white pickup with the official seal of the law. They toyed with his body, kicked him a few times in the back, not mean kicks, just doing what looked right, fingering his pockets and divvying up his money. He felt sticky weeds and hot exhaust from the truck on his cheek. He checked his crotch for the hidden money and rolled farther into the ditch, warmer here, and he imagined a pool of blue water opening up for him.

CHAPTER THIRTY-SIX

LA COCA BROKE THEIR record tonight and scrambled ten eggs at once, cooking them with extra oil, a bit of green onion, a single diced tomato. Hernán, who had once pulled the warm eggs from beneath their hens in Cuturú, knew the butcher got his product from a giant factory of drugged hens in cages, laying everything of the same size, color, consistency, with no idea about the look of the world, the touch of dirt on their claws, a cat to watch out for.

"I could eat nothing but eggs the rest of my life." Hernán picked up his plate and licked at the cold grease.

"You'd go crazy," la Coca said. "Besides, your tongue would lose its taste buds, and your head would grow bigger and turn into an egg."

A summer night at the center of winter. She leaned back against the empty water tank, and Hernán kissed her. All around him he could hear the day dying down, the dogs scratching their necks, the children ending their play prematurely and hoping for dinner. The neighborhood was busy with its problems, not about street corners and lines between sectors, the apparent cause of recent gang killings, but about the lack of water.

"No one remembers your robbery," she said, putting his hands on her belly. "You were not meant to be killed. Soon you'll know how you did on the exam, and then—"

Just the thought of those fluorescent lights burning into his eyes, the rows of confident bogotanos, their hair long and skin light, as they chatted about what neighborhood they lived in, what band they liked, where and what they might study, until the proctor handed out the tests. Hernán had wondered how many points he might get for writing his name and ID number correctly, and then the first math question was very hard, then a few easy ones, and then he pushed through the dense word problems, the data, the graphs, the grammar and sentences, paragraphs with problems, with secrets, and him staring so hard at his paper, the five possible answers.

"It couldn't have gone bad," she said. "You got better grades than Cate. You studied hard."

"Don't talk about it, mi amor. Just wait."

They were sitting at the red plastic table, and the thing they didn't say was that Antonio was dead. The blue vest la Coca wore to sell calls hung on a nail above the bed. She had gotten a new phone from her father Riki, but she was too heavy and close to birth to be working.

Hernán twisted the dial of the radio, tapping the antenna against the brick wall.

"Is it broken?"

"Let's keep it off to hear the water."

"We'll hear it. No one is deaf here."

With a soft touch, la Coca found the clear emission of salsa. Her breasts hung without a bra in a white V-neck shirt too small for her immense stomach. She put him on edge with her new beauty, as if a distant cousin of the girl who used to have a black scab on her thumb, bad makeup, bad clothes, sitting on the soccer court and making a scene about some no-name doll.

Antonio's mother had stopped by earlier to confirm that his corpse had been identified in a ditch outside Ocana. She was stoic about it, her head cocked far sideways and her lips bitten to a raw

gray color. She blamed Marta, the rich uphill puta he had been trying to please. She said that the sooner the bodies piled up, the better.
She knew Antonio deserved it, but not dressed up as a guerrillero so
President Uribe could brag. Today they had interviewed her on television, and she lied and said he was a good boy, he cleaned the house,
he threw crates each morning at Abastos, and gave her money. She
lied because it was easier. She told them how he used to talk to the
seagulls, to the sun, how he was sensitive, and he believed in God.
Tomorrow she would go with other Cazucá mothers to protest outside the city hall in Soacha. She would show a picture of him smiling
with his lips together to cover his bad teeth.

I almost went with him, Hernán had told her, and she kissed his
hair and said he was too intelligent to die.

He was a good friend to me, la Coca said without lying. He gave
me clothes for nothing, underwear, socks, when Riki was gone and
we were low on money. He was thoughtful. He stole, but he was
always generous. No one around here gives anything to anyone.

We're going to bury him on Sunday, Antonio's mother said.
Please, come. He was so popular in this neighborhood, so respected.
But what if no one goes?

Now, as they had eaten dinner, as the night was not cold, their
mood was giddy, and la Coca made Hernán stand up to dance.
When she went too fast, he grabbed her waist and said, "The baby."

At the end of each song they went to the patio to check for water,
and la Coca put a rubber hose in her ear to listen for it. All of el
Progreso had suffered a dry two weeks. Every afternoon the emergency tank truck from Bogotá parked by the soccer court, quickly
surrounded by children and teenagers with buckets and bottles.
Hernán hated the weight of water, too proud to carry much across
the causeway, then four blocks up the steepest part of la Gran Vía.

When it came, the neighbors would bash their pans together and
whistle. Maybe it would last long enough to fill the two tanks on

the patio, or time to fill every plastic bag, bottle, cup, in the house—even spray it across the walls and floor to get rid of the dust.

"Are you on your way?" la Coca said to the dry rubber hose. "Let's dance again."

"Too tired," he said.

"And I stink. I'm the one who sold minutes all day. You have no right. What *did* we eat?"

"Eggs! You have a big one here."

He reached out, but she dodged him. Salsa kept playing. He cornered her against the wall and kissed her.

"Let me go," she said, which meant she wanted to be bound.

"Stand still!" He found a T-shirt and tied her to a little red chair and the red table, and the interrogation began. "They say you carry a special baby. True?"

"It's true."

She worked tears into her eyes, thinking of sad things—Antonio dead, her mother muzzled with a sock and tape, tied to the bed and beaten by Riki who then brought roasted chickens and criollo potatoes from Soacha, promising money for school, a move off the hill, as soon as they confessed their betrayal. She stared up at the rusty waves of steel and cried.

"Poor mamá," she said.

"Agua, señores!" a neighbor yelled, as the neighbors bashed their pots. "Agua! Hurry! Cuánto va a durar? How long will it last? Who knows?"

They rushed onto the patio and shoved the hose into the tank. They tasted it, and Hernán discarded in his mind the rumors of the government poisoning the water to keep poor people stupid. It tasted fine.

"Should we risk it?" she said. "I'm so dirty."

"Undress."

"Are you sure?"

"Vamos. Dale, cochina."

"Hurry. I'm freezing."

Water glanced off her oily hair, her strong shoulders, into a pool at her feet. She was built of dust. He tried to hand her the bar of soap, but she closed her eyes, moaned, and so he ran it down her neck, scrubbing along the canal of her spine, around the dome of her belly and between her toes, his other hand high above him with the hose. It had never flowed so well. Uphill, he heard the explosion of hoses leaping off their spouts and the curses of the neighbors.

La Coca ran dripping for the bed.

"It's my turn," he said. "Get up."

"I'm so tired. Hold it for yourself."

"I held it for you."

"Mi amor! I'm pregnant. Let me rest."

He found the soap in a puddle of mud, cleaned it, and covered his body with gauzy white foam. He held the hose over his back. The shock of cold stole his breath for a second. It was not easy alone, but one needed to be macho, and he shivered, hugging himself, reciting decade by decade the events of Colombian history, as if he were about to take the exam again. At the end of the history, Antonio disguised as a dead guerrillero in a ditch.

CHAPTER THIRTY-SEVEN

THEY GOT OFF TOGETHER at la avenida 19, walked up la avenida Jiménez. Hernán showed her the spots where he and Wilfredo used to sell. Alba looked at the walkers as if she were the only sane person on the avenue. She sat purposefully and smoked one of the blue Mustang cigarettes, ashing into the fountain, spitting, and babbling about the smell of frying fish up those alleyways, how next week when she got paid, they would come again and eat a fish soup among the suits and rich students. Her voice had turned from a smooth reed to a victim's whine; it brought inside it the cruelties done to her, and flung back at the world a new way of being, outspoken, grating.

"Do you think we'll find him today?" she said.

"I doubt it."

He took one of her cigarettes and sat next to her. In the sun, her brownish hair was lit like a piece of rusted roofing. How could he ever interfere with her drama of loyalty? She would find Wilfredo somehow, and what she found might be better than if he were to knock on the door tonight and ask into her bed.

"You were your father's son," she said. "I told him you could be a panguero, too, but he said, No, he'll be an engineer. He'll go away and come back elegant. Milton will stay, he said. How could we know?"

When she stood up and wandered the blocks between la avenida

Jiménez and the presidential Palacio Nariño, Hernán went to ride buses. He asked passengers for a second of their time. He told them about his studies, his hope to go to la Universidad Nacional, how his girlfriend was pregnant. "Any coin suits us," he would say, and God would pay them back for it. If He did not, it was because they owed too much. "Laugh, damas y caballeros. Not everything has to be serious. I will accept any coin as an act of love."

He would walk the aisle back and forth until the driver threw him off or a few passengers, regardless of his speech, would press a coin or two into his palm, enough for some lunch and bus fare back to Cazucá, but never enough for la Coca. He changed his story depending on his audience, his mood, the sector of the city. As he went south of el centro, the stories had to place the poor against the rich because these people were inured to the usual tragedies. Today, he found himself on a bus weaving through the garment district of Restrepo. "I was a brilliant student at the best school in my district," he told them. "I learned all they gave me and I took the government exam, and I might have broken a record for the lowest score ever by an arrogant pendejo from Cazucá. And what? They taught me the wrong material. How is that fair, señores y señoras? Por favor, we could use your help."

On a different bus, he told the story about Antonio whom General Montoya of the armed forces had labeled a falso positivo, an innocent civilian "mistakenly" classified as a guerrillero killed in combat. "The soldiers carried him into the mountains and shot him."

"Your friend was up to no good anyway," said a woman with a tall black wig. "What did he expect?"

At this point the bus driver was rapping a crowbar against the plastic divider. Not a single peso had been offered, and so Hernán would have to stop talking about Antonio and focus on his education.

For Alba, there was some pleasure in surveying the spaces where

Wilfredo had been. She was not after the thing she thought, but something else that could only have value as long as she was ignorant of it. Maybe her life was directed in this way, possessed by a certain unknown desire, while fulfilling, unconsciously, a greater task. It consoled her to think this.

Alba had kept her position at the factory and gave money to Lidia during Ramón's absence, allowing the albino to have his fun. In Station 12, the loading dock, she carried out the simple task of stacking and packaging the plastic with another young woman, both of them so fast the line could not keep up, so that they had to maintain just the right rhythm to look busy. It gave Alba time to watch men move in Abastos, one of them perhaps Wilfredo. She rooted for the throwers, for the sellers who duped the grocers and chefs and stingy women and men who lived in the city, whose children went to school and did not beg on buses. Time passed slower away from the line. Her back hurt from the lifting, and something about the cardboard, the glue they used, caused pink-black sores to erupt on the backs of her hands. Maybe it was the semen that irritated her skin. The albino liked to catch her by surprise, to slam the door on that section of the assembly line—shooing away the other woman—and push Alba into some boxes, undress her, turn her around and admire her defective body in the cool light of the doorway. But he did not touch her, and she began to wish that he would. That's why he doesn't get tired of it, Cintia said. If you touch him, then it's over.

Maybe so, but Alba was getting prettier, her skin tanned a vivid brown, her arms muscular, her legs veiny and lumpy, but who cared in the capital where all the legs were concealed in pants. It was her face. Carved around her shocked eyes was a new face of edges, of an unlikely wisdom, as if God or her mind had finally decided that if she was not going to bleed to death from a pregnancy or get her throat stabbed through by a paramilitary, she may as well find some pleasure in life. She was the only one who did not see her beauty.

She saw nothing but her missing chin, perhaps the most beautiful part of her.

Alba often caught Wilfredo boarding buses just out of her reach or looking out the window of one, beside him the whore, the younger woman who did not blame him for her losses, perhaps a maid, a baker, a peddler, but a whore for sure. Today, though, looking up as she had taught herself to do, she saw him framed in the window of an office building, and she waved him down to the street. He was close. The walkers cruised past with incurious gazes, wishing she could be insane in private, yet knowing that there was not space in the capital for everyone to break down alone. So, go ahead, their looks said. Lose your shit.

He disappeared behind the window. She tried to gain entrance but could not get past the front door without an appointment, and the security guard knew of no Wilfredo.

She waited, and Hernán arrived with some coffee and waited too. He did not believe. She knew from his look he was thinking about la Coca, and she wanted to tell him that this was love.

"Let's go visit Milton," he said, "and then go home. It's late. It's still not safe for me."

"Just a few more minutes," she said, for it was dusk and lights came on in the buildings. "Just to confirm I saw him."

Hernán bought some cheap bananas from a peddler and ate one, handed her the other. She peeled it carefully, never taking her eye off the door. While the city went dark, her skin turned to bronze, something he could not help but touch, dragging his thumb along one of the gummy white scars on the back of her forearm. He had never seen Alba in this light. She had always been afflicted. He ate a second banana and felt his stomach fill. She too ate another, putting the four peels in a pile on the street.

"We don't even have to see Milton," he said, "if you are tired."

"No. If we don't go, we'll forget who he is."

Milton would be wearing his beige uniform with a badge, with black shoulder stripes, a .44 Magnum Colt revolver buttoned to his hip, in a building with a botanical atrium in the center, where bamboo and ferns grew in just a shaft of light from the ceiling and water trickled past in a gray stream. Milton had to walk around the hallways in their entirety every half hour, surveying for irregularities, and the sound of his heels clicking on the tiles, combined with the sound of the stream, put the residents at ease. His look had changed too. He had the mouth of an ass-kisser, his head bowed slightly, his hair buzzed. He never gave Alba any of his money, at least not enough to make a difference. He was getting back at her, she knew, for leaving him behind with Tuts.

Alba and Hernán materialized in the big glass door. A resident and the two policemen who protected a senator were chatting with Milton who saw his family and seemed embarrassed. He noted the yellow dust in their clothes and their worn-out shoes, unbuttoned his gun, and told his partner to cover his post.

The three of them walked up the street to a bakery a block from his building, bending over to choose from a tray of greasy pastries and sitting on stools in the window. They faced the street, and their own images, thin, disintegrating, faced them back.

"It's cold," Alba said, just to say something. "I miss the heat of Cuturú. I think about all the treasures you brought home, Hernán. You were a little crazy."

"The junk," Milton said.

To imagine such heat from here, in a light mist, seeing nothing but edges of brick and glass, the sky blocked by smoke and scaffolding, was to split their lives in two.

"Tuts is dead," Milton said. "I got a call, who knows why me, but they said he lost control of a saw and sliced his leg off. He hopped to a bus stop and bled to death. Too cheap to call an ambulance. Hijo de puta."

"He was very cheap," Alba said. "It wasn't how he expected it. No guerrilla."

"He was not a good teacher," Milton said. "Look. I have a camera in my cell phone."

It flipped open with a screen that moved. He snapped a picture of Alba before she was ready, and she looked at her feet, blushing. He took one of Hernán who stared impatiently, chewing through a piece of fatty beef within the fried bread. Then they squeezed together by the counter, the two smaller heads of the boys sandwiching Alba's, and although no one smiled, you could see in their faces the potential for love. He snapped another and then flipped it shut, patting it safe within his pocket.

"Wilfredo will turn up, maybe," Alba said after she had finished her own pastry, which was filled with gelatinous fruit. "He'll want to bury Tuts. We could travel. I can't find him on my own around here."

"No," Milton said. "I can't get the time."

"La Coca," Hernán said. "She's too close."

"Then no one will go," she said. "Who will bury Tuts?"

They watched the street and leaned their elbows against the glass, past the time when it was safe for Alba and Hernán to walk up the hill into Cazucá, past when Milton should have gotten back to make his walk-around. He straightened his guard hat in the mirror, adjusted his holster, his tie. On the street, he kissed Alba, promising to visit, though he never would, and walked up the steep hill. "Until soon," he said. "Poor Tuts."

"Poor Tuts," Alba said, as they walked down long blocks of apartment buildings, pointing at the two-story buildings where they might like to live someday, and crossed on a pedestrian bridge to a busy corner. Alba still watched for Wilfredo in the faces of the bus passengers.

"We'll find him next week," Hernán said.

La Coca was probably sitting with the medical dictionary or one of the encyclopedias, while in the other room Antonio's television blathered about soft drinks and vacations and cold medicines. She would tell him what she had learned. She did not see the patterns in the histories and ideas she read about, nor the connection between her own fate and that of the conquerors, the subjects, but she used them to make her life into a story. A week ago, when he had been sick in bed, depressed by his results on the exam, she came with a cup of water and a toothbrush. She was gentle, sliding the coarse bristles up along his gums, along his cheeks and tongue, to clean every tooth. He rinsed with water and spit into the cup, and she kissed him. That was all.

CHAPTER THIRTY-EIGHT

I N H O S P I T A L S A N P E L A Y O in Soacha, Hernán weaved his way between the gurneys, the bleeding patients, the anemic, the pregnant, the amputees, the yellow-faced, and tried to find a phone to call Lidia. Loud machines beeped and pulsed; nurses called for help or joked with each other, while a young boy, who seemed to have flown through a windshield, cried insanely from the board he was strapped to.

Marta answered, and she was not excited to hear from him. She said she would fetch Lidia at La Esperanza, leave a note for Alba who would be home any minute, and that Caterín was also supposed to visit. "I can't go," she said. "My baby is sick, and the wind is cold today. I'm sorry. Tell la Coca it will end." The mark of Marta's teeth still stood out pink on the back of la Coca's neck, and neither of them had gone to see her baby since they had moved back into the cantina house. The baby was unwell and carried the name of Antonio.

"How long?" Hernán said, returning to the room where a nurse with a comically large head and tiny uneven shoulders, a white wart on the edge of her chin, was looking between la Coca's knees. The nurse and her wart, her gravitas, her sure hands, made him feel too young to have a baby, and it scared him.

"How long?" he repeated.

"Leave!" la Coca said. "Leave if you can't handle it, pendejo! Mierda!"

"Can you give her a drug?" Hernán said. "She's crazy."

"Don't drug me!" la Coca said. "I want to feel it."

The nurse was in no hurry to speak or follow directions. She was in a hurry to pull back the green curtains and go to other rooms, to continue on her rounds. She had no time to sit with la Coca and stare at her dilating cervix. La Coca was not ready. It might be an hour, it might be three, the nurse explained, lifting up her hands in a useless gesture to signal time, its unknown quality, the hand of fate that would move their baby.

"Is it good or bad if it takes a long time?" Hernán said.

"What?" the nurse said. "What? Be happy she has a bed. Look around. I'm not God. I can't do anything to change this." She touched his arm, but she was talking through him to la Coca who, tangled up already in the yellow gown, was kicking the air with crooked feet, the soles a grayish-yellow, campesino feet, a picker, a planter, a bananera with jagged calluses on her big toes. He reached out and pressed his thumbs into the soft, veiny arches. He pulled them down to the cheap plastic mattress, the sheets upset, undone, and he pulled everything taut and tucked in the edges.

"I'll be back soon," the nurse said, dipping her smaller shoulder through the curtain and hurrying off.

"I'm dying," la Coca said. "It's certain."

She was not breathing like Caterín had taught her. She was holding her air in and swallowing, as if to drive more pain into her gut, staring past him at a hole in the ceiling, bracing for the next contraction.

"I called Lidia," he said. "Marta told me to tell you that it will end."

"Shut up," she said. "Don't touch me."

"What do you want? Do you want water?"

"Did you tell her to call my mother?"

"Yes," he lied.

"What did she say?"

"She said she'd call. Is your mother home now?"

"What? Please, stop. Shut your mouth. I can hardly breathe with you talking. And it's loud here. Why did we not go to the hospital in Kennedy? We are in the worst hospital in the whole country. I don't feel safe. Dios mío. Can you plug my ears?"

"With what?"

"Help me!"

He brought some Kleenex from the nurse station and twisted little twigs of it into her ears, but then she slapped his hand away and pulled them out, asking him if he was trying to break her ears. He stood back and watched her suffer. He had seen the solution on TV, a dripping syringe in the soft arm of a woman, dragging her gently into the soft consciousness of a gray-misted room, and her pain just a bland rumor, a wince in the eyes of the others.

"Maybe if you ask for medicine," he said.

"No!"

He shifted foot to foot, leaning on the bed, seeing past her feet to the inflamed labia, a spot of light for the baby who might be ready. The baby, he thought, would look at him and see a man, not a kid. It wouldn't know the difference. Hernán searched for authority in his voice. "Carmen," he said to la Coca. "Mi amor. Patience. It could be hours and so you have to breathe more and think about somewhere else. Think about Boyacá and snow in the mountains."

"Talk to me," she said, hiccuping with pain, one foot weaving a loop in the air. "Don't leave. Just talk to me. Tell me something, not a story, just about a place and not around here."

"Tranquila. Boyacá. Boyacá is . . ."

"No, not Boyacá! A place you know!"

"Cuturú . . ."

A man screamed past their curtain, catching it on the edge of his gurney, a number of nurses holding him flat while a doctor shoved a giant syringe into his bloody back. The gurney crashed into the wall, and the doctor was swearing at the nurses, at all the people crowding the hospital.

"Go," la Coca said, "if you have nothing good to say."

"Excuse me," a nurse said, this one tiny but fast, pretty, already pulling at la Coca's bed and shoving him aside. "We need this space. And you, señor, have to go. The doctor wants all the visitors to leave."

The doctor pulled back the curtain and smiled. He was young with long black sideburns and a trustworthy face. "Wait," he said. His eyes were sickly. "Hola, Carmen," he said, looking at her wristband and then pulling up her gown. "Muy bien. I am Doctor Suárez. You are close. Everything is normal."

"Can I stay?" Hernán said.

"We'll call you. Look around at this mess. I'm sorry."

*

There were no open seats and hardly a standing space in the waiting room. No plants, no pictures, and the air did not move, unless someone opened the door and even then it was just a wind of gasoline smoke. The doors back through the emergency room were automatic, controlled by a nurse behind a thick sheet of glass. Hernán walked an embarrassed circle around the center of the room, and the unadmitted patients stared as if he were returning with news from the world of medicine, checking his eyes for the doctors and nurses and metallic instruments and cures he had seen. One woman, her arm wrapped up in a dirty T-shirt, seeming badly broken, moaned in synchronization with a man gripping his testicles from a crawling position next to the door, no chair for him either. The patients competed with each other, comparing the times of their waits, to win the prize of worst neglect, for pity, for something to say. They asked Hernán about the inside, and he said it was crowded. He said it was not much better, but they did not believe it. Why should they? Why keep waiting if there was nothing behind the doors? At this they became weary and bored with the sight of him and turned back to a television that showed a street corner in Bogotá where a woman was launching pots of boiling water out her window on top of the policemen who had come to evict her; her neighbors cheered her on, and the patients' eyes glinted with approval.

He went outside to breathe. The sun had just set. Soacha was as loud as the hospital, in heavy evening traffic, an ambulance plowing through the middle of it. He lit a cigarette. He could see some lights on the distant hill and its familiar pattern. He wished Antonio were here, for he would know what to say, never worried, and, despite his ugliness, he would charm the nurses. He would not be asked to leave. Hernán found himself waiting, just as his father had waited for Alba to lose each of her babies. What if la Coca were bleeding, asking for help and getting none?

In the distance, he saw Lidia step out of a taxi with her starchy, full moon-face, then Alba, Caterín, even Ramón and Marta with her baby. Hernán felt small. They were looking for a father, and they saw only him with his cigarette, not knowing where to stand or what to say. They looked up at the filthy, impenetrable windows of the black hospital, through the mix of people in the entrance, the automatic door clicking open and closing.

"She's close," he said.

"You should be inside," Caterín said. Her hair was newly cut in the strange, crooked way of the indigenous, popular now among girls at la Universidad Nacional. "You should watch."

"They threw me out."

"They can't. Vamos. I'll talk."

Marta pulled down the neck of her sweatshirt and gave her breast to tiny Antonio who had no hair, just a dry face with pink spots on his forehead, little aimless hands jutting out for anything. Hernán squeezed his little foot. He looked at Alba who smelled like plastic, who wrapped her arm around his waist and told him his baby would be healthy and talented and he should get ready for the responsibility. Ramón glared at her, at Lidia, at everything, rubbing his face with the back of his hand, for through the opening door of the emergency room he saw what he most despised: poverty. But he was here, a part of them.

So they entered, all of them, eventually finding their way back into the corridors of the sick and the cured and the incurable.

ACKNOWLEDGMENTS

I thank Ron Carlson for seeing this book start, for his patience, encouragement, and smart advice; Michelle Latiolais for all her love and passion for literature, for the immense support she has given me; Christine Schutt for her sincerity and intensity, her kindness, for the books she has written; the poet Will Schutt for the time he spent on these lines; my UC Irvine workshop colleagues and friends who endured and embraced this project, always critical, always encouraging and helpful, in particular Alberto Gullaba, Ryan Ridge, Jen Began, Kim O'Neil, and Matt Nelson; Jim McMichael and Michael Ryan for all they taught me about writing; and Deb Olin Unferth and Mike Levine for their great help in revising and bringing this book into print.

All my love to María, my wife, who found a piece of this novel on my desk, read it, and told me it had potential.